ZENOBIA JULY

ZENOBIA JULY

Lisa Bunker

VIKING

VIKING
An imprint of Penguin Random House LLC, New York

First published in the United States of America by Viking,
an imprint of Penguin Random House LLC, 2019

Visit us online at penguinrandomhouse.com

LIBRARY OF CONGRESS CATALOGING-IN-PUBLICATION DATA IS AVAILABLE.
ISBN 9780451479402

Printed in the USA   Set in Goudy Old Style   Book design by Jim Hoover

10   9   8   7   6   5   4   3   2   1

In memory of Leelah Alcorn

and of all the other children

who couldn't find a way through.

This book was born out of pondering

what needed to be different

in order for you to endure and survive.

ONE

SHE HAD THAT new kid look. Anyone paying attention could have seen it. In the flinchiness of her shoulders. In the way her eyes skittered from face to face as the other students streamed past. Managed to show up, her shoulders and eyes said, but not sure about having the nerve to actually go in. Might be too much today.

Not that anyone was paying attention. First day of school at Monarch Middle, everyone was scoping for friends, shouting hey, clustering up. It was a hot morning. It felt like summer swearing it was going to stick around this year, no really. The wind moving through the high branches of the trees made wavering leaf shadows.

The new kid was wearing a blue dress that was too big for her, sneakers with white socks pushed down, and a heavy-looking backpack. Her jumbled mopflop of hair made her face look smaller and her eyes look bigger. The tiny metal balls that ear-piercers put in newly pierced ears glinted in her lobes. She hovered behind a pillar at the far end of the entrance, away from the crush.

Fewer students now, mostly single ones hurrying to beat the bell. Each time the metal-and-glass doors swung shut, a mirror image of the sidewalk clunked back into place, and each time, the new kid's eyes shifted toward it. She looked like she might be asking her reflection to tell her that everything was going to be all right. But then her eyes always went down again, like maybe her reflection had shaken its head.

Now a minute with no one using the leftmost door. This time her eyes stayed. She stared at her mirror image.

She turned first to one side, then the other. She swished her dress.

A furtive glance around, and then an awkward pirouette. As she finished the spin a truck passed behind her, turning the reflection background dark and transparent, and she screened her face with her hands and cringed away. Someone was watching her through the glass.

The door opened and the watcher came out—another student. What you might notice first, if you were a detail person: the sharp-edged exact haircut with a part. The stocky, square body shape. The jeans rolled up to mid calf, revealing mismatched socks, the button-down shirt and boots, the big black glasses. Or, if you were more the general-impression type, you might notice that this new person seemed equally balanced between looking like a girl and looking like a boy.

The watcher approached cautiously, stopped a few steps away. "Hey. You okay?"

No answer.

"Um . . . I haven't seen you before. Are you new?"

Still no answer, just an eyes-wide look. But then, one quick nod.

"Oh. Okay." Silence. "Um, so, you wanna come inside? School is about to start."

The new kid curled sideways like she was trying to disappear into herself. The bell rang. Her body jerked.

"You don't say much." Not mean, just saying.

The skin around those big eyes got wrinkles in it. "I can talk." Just above a whisper, but clear enough.

"Cool. You can dance, too. Looked good. Nice moves."

The new kid's fingers twisted together.

"So, person who can talk and dance, do you also have a name?"

Again the new kid tried to curl-disappear, so hard she stumbled back around. After a couple of seconds, though, her head came up and her spine got straight again and she turned back. "My name is Zenobia." A little gasp after, like it had taken all her strength to say.

"What? No way! How do you spell that?"

Zenobia spelled her name.

"And what's your last name?" The question was eager,

almost hard, but it came with a light in the eyes. Some kind of geeky glee happening there.

"My last name?"

"Yeah."

Silence. Then, "July." An actual whisper this time.

"Like the month?"

"Yes. My name is Zenobia July." Another gasp.

A sudden laugh. Geeky glee stronger now, beaming out. "That is totally Ex. Cell. Ent! Eleven letters and no repeats."

Zen's eyes went up and left. For a second, picturing alphabet, she forgot to look scared. "You're right," she said. "I never noticed."

"That's the closest anyone has come in a long time to matching me. But you didn't, not quite. I've got thirteen."

"Thirteen letters?"

"Uh-huh."

"With no repeats."

"Yeah."

Zen waited, then asked, sounding just a little annoyed. "Okay then, so what's your name?"

"Arli, people call me. A-R-L-I."

"That's only four letters."

"No duh."

"So what's your full name?"

"Yeah, you know what? I'm already late for class. Find

me at lunch and ask me again then. You coming in?"

Zen's eyes did another circuit: school entrance, down at herself, then up again to Arli's face. For the first time, a touch of a smile. "Yeah, okay, I guess I can. Thanks." They went in together through the mirrored door.

TWO

ZEN FELT HERSELF whirled along like a twig in a flood, her mind battered by the flurry and racket and smell of so many other kids. And the eyes. So many eyes. Teachers garbled at her, and she nodded and agreed to whatever it was they had said. Only one thing kept her from giving in to the overwhelm. It was a silly thing, but even as she rolled her eyes at it she grabbed the lifeline: she wanted to know Arli's full name. Just hang on till lunch, she whispered to herself. Just hang on till lunch.

Before lunch, though, there was another challenge to get through: bathroom break. On the way into her second-period class, she spotted the door to the girls' restroom a short stretch down the hall. During the last five minutes of class she packed up her things, and then the instant the bell rang she was out the door, down the hall, first person in the room, and straight into the farthest stall.

It took a second to remember to lift the dress up instead

of pulling it down. As she settled on the cool plastic of the seat she checked sight lines through the cracks. Nothing but wall, except all the way to the right a bit of the last sink. If anyone was going to peek they'd have to come down to the end, and there was no reason, with the last stall taken. She was as safe as she could expect to be. She sat and tried to still her quivering body enough to let go and relieve her aching bladder.

Just as the squeezer muscles down there finally began to relax, the door creaked and footsteps entered. Her squeezer muscles clamped shut again.

". . . hair like that," Voice Number One was saying.

"God, I know, right?" said Voice Number Two.

"It looked like, you know, when they're selling pumpkins at Halloween? Like scarecrow hair made of, you know, corn husks. Corn husk hair."

Giggles. "God, Natalie, you're so *mean*," said Voice Number Two admiringly.

"Just calling it the way I see it," said Voice Number One, aka Natalie apparently. Natalie talked like she was Queen of the World.

Zen bent double and buried her face in her knees. Girl-voices echoed between hard surfaces, but she couldn't hear the words anymore. The door creaked again. Feet grouped and shuffled. The five minutes of class-break took a year to pass. Only when the bell had rung and the room had emptied again would her squeezer muscles finally unclench. She was late for her third class.

Two endless class periods later another bell rang, and Zen checked her sweat-creased schedule for the twentieth time. Yes, she had made it. Lunch. The cafeteria was still going to be a gauntlet—all those eyes, all in one place—but at least if Arli was there, there would be one face she had seen before.

The haircut and glasses were easy to spot. Arli was sitting at an edge table with a couple of other kids, one of them a girl wearing a colorful head scarf pinned at her chin, the other a seriously skinny boy with a buzz cut on one side of his head and long bright-blue hair on the other, tied back in a half ponytail. Zen clutched the reusable lunch bag Aunt Phil had given her and wove her way over.

Arli looked up as she approached. "Hey. Join us."

"Thanks." She sat down. The two kids she didn't know yet looked at her. Zen ducked her face.

Half-and-half hair boy spoke. "Hi. Welcome to Arli's table of orphan misfits. I'm Clem."

"Orphans?"

"Not literally."

"Clem?"

"Arli gave me that. Nickname Genius over here."

"But, why Clem?"

"It's short for Clementine. I had one in my lunch the day we met. My regular boring name is Greg."

"Oh." All three still looking at her. She swallowed, made herself go on. "Okay, my name is—"

Arli cut in. "Zen." Said like it was a Moment.

"Um, yes? That is what I was going to say?"

"And now there's no turning back," said Clem. "Now you're one of us."

"But . . . that's so obvious."

Arli did a stare over glasses. "So?"

"And my aunts already use it."

"So? Sometimes simple is best. Do not question the Nickname Genius."

Zen turned to the other girl. "Um, so, what did Arli name you?"

"Dyna. It is short for Dynamo." She said the last word with a push, like the announcer in a superhero cartoon, and Arli and Clem laughed. "What is funny?" said Dyna. She had an accent.

Clem touched her arm. "Nothing. We love you."

"Oh? Okay." She turned back to Zen. "My real name is Chantal."

Zen glanced at Arli. "So why Dyna?" she said.

"Because she has such intense eyes." She did, indeed—a sharp, bright, steady gaze.

"I like your scarf," Zen said. It was the first thing she had said all day just because she was thinking it. The scarf was partly plain black, but with a border of gold and purple in an elaborate print design.

Dyna smiled. "*Merci*, thank you," she said.

"*De rien*, you're welcome," said Clem, looking pleased with himself. Language geek, maybe.

"Hijab," said Arli. Word geek, already established.

"Yes," said Dyna. "You remember."

Dyna's smile gave Zen the courage to speak her curiosity. "Where are you from?"

"From the Democratic Republic of the Congo. Here two years."

Clem said, "Where are *you* from, Zen? Only fair."

"Oh. Um, Arizona. Here, um, four months."

"How come you moved to the beautiful city of Portland, Maine?"

A reasonable question, but Zen's eyes went down and her body folded into itself. Trying to disappear again. Glances among the other three. Arli said, "Never mind. Some other time, right?"

"Sure," said Clem. Dyna nodded.

To get past the moment, Zen unpacked the lunch Aunt Phil had made for her. It turned out to be a couple of plastic tubs, one containing cut-up veggies, the other full of brownish-yellow goop. She popped the lid and garlic-smell puffed up hard. So many new foods since coming to live with the Aunties. She had seen this one before, but she couldn't remember what it was called. "What is this again?" she asked.

Three pairs of eyes examined her lunch.

"Hummus?" said Dyna.

"Looks like," said Clem. "Haven't you ever seen hummus before?"

"Not often enough to remember the name."

Arli said, "How can you not know hummus? It's the official state dip of Arizona." The other two laughed, and after a second Zen did too . . . and just like that, they were joking around, the way friends do. The conversation veered randomly, it didn't matter where, and Zen ate her veggies and hummus, and lunch period passed easy.

It was only when the bell rang that she realized she still didn't know Arli's full name. "Give me your number," Arli said. "I'll text you." Then it was time for class.

THREE

THE AFTERNOON STILL blurred by, but it wasn't as bad as before. Now underneath all the spinning, Zen felt a floor, because now there were three faces she might see that she knew. Clem's blue hair made him easy to spot, and she did, twice, once with eye contact and an eyebrow flash. And Dyna turned out to be in her last-period class. There were no empty seats near her when Zen came in, but they exchanged friendly looks, and it helped. Arli she did not see again, but Arli had her phone number. There were connections now. New reasons on the yes side of the question of whether it was possible she might actually survive this.

When the last bell finally rang and the hall-flow spilled Zen out in front of the school, she saw Aunt Phil in the park across the street . . . talking to a squirrel? That seemed to be what she was doing. Zen bit her lip. Aunt Phil was definitely an odd person, and Zen hadn't yet figured out how to feel completely comfortable with her.

Aunt Phil had a craggy face and big, gnarled hands and a clumpy-stumpy way of moving around in her boots and jeans. She also had a wild Mohawk-style haircut, dyed red, orange, and yellow, and rows of rings all the way up around both ears. And, she talked like hippie was definitely still a thing.

But it was Aunt Phil's eyes that most alarmed Zen. Alarmed, but also intrigued. They were so bright, and you got the sense when they looked at you that you were being *seen*. Zen had spent most of her life looking into eyes that were closed off like the doors of vaults, or roiling with anger, or both. After so many eyes like that, it was hard to look steadily back into Aunt Phil's shrewd twinkle.

Oh, and, one more thing: Aunt Phil used pet names. A seemingly endless variety of them. Zen hadn't yet decided how she felt about that.

She crossed the street and walked under the park trees to join her aunt, who was, indeed, talking to a squirrel. "Nice chatting with you, little critter," she said as Zen stepped close. "But I gotta wind it up now. My girl is out." Then that disconcerting gaze, and, "Well, hey, pumpkin. You made it."

"Yes, ma'am."

Aunt Phil gave her a look, and Zen blushed red. The Aunties had asked her, politely but firmly, several times, not to call them "ma'am." She was trying, but it was hard training to break. "Take two?" said Aunt Phil gently.

"Yes . . . thanks. I made it."

A smile. "Right on. Good for you."

Zen returned the smile.

"Any less than stellar aspects of the day?"

"Um . . . no, not really. Just a lot of people. I'm not used to it."

"Yeah, right on. So many humans. I dig that."

"And there was a tricky part in a bathroom."

"Oh, heavy," Aunt Phil said, nodding.

"But it turned out fine."

"Groovy." Another smile.

Zen looked back across the street to see if anyone was watching. "Um, you didn't have to come get me. I remember how to get back to your apartment."

"Our."

"I'm sorry, what?"

"Our apartment. It's yours, too, now. You know that, right?"

"Yes, m— Um, okay, thanks." Growing more aware of the possibility of watching eyes, Zen started pull-stepping toward home. Aunt Phil obliged, and they were headed back. The apartment was only a few blocks away, up in the old Parkside neighborhood.

Zen said, "You still didn't have to come get me."

"Sure, I dig. Like this morning, all independent. But I just wanted to make sure our wandering lamb was okay, okay?"

Zen glanced up at the rugged face. Those eyes glinted back, full of a sort of gleeful mischief. "Okay?" Aunt Phil repeated.

"Okay. Thanks." They walked in silence for a minute. "Tomorrow, I want to come back alone."

"Right on. Groovy. Gotcha. And what a gorgeous blue it is, the sky today, don't you think? You could flip gravity upside down and just dive straight up into it."

Aunt Phil worked in a restaurant kitchen, so she was home a lot during the day. Aunt Lucy, who was Zen's actual aunt, her father's older sister, was a professor at the local university. She was a tall woman, very thin, with short gray hair. If there was a pattern to Aunt Lucy's coming and going, Zen hadn't figured it out yet. She was in the apartment when they arrived. "Welcome home, Zenobia," said Aunt Lucy. "I'm glad to see you. How did it go?"

"It went fine, thanks."

"She had some kind of bathroom conundrum to figure out, I guess," said Aunt Phil.

Aunt Lucy was instantly intent. Her eyes had a different kind of sharpness to them. The way they flashed, it seemed like she was always ready for a fight. "What happened?"

"Nothing. I just got scared."

"Scared of what?"

"Oh, I don't know. Stupid stuff. Nothing anybody said or did, to me anyway. I spent the whole break in the stall, and these girls were talking about someone. Saying mean things."

"Ah, indeed," said Aunt Lucy. "That would be part of the novelty of the day, of course it would. First substantive inside encounter with American girl culture. Quite apart from the challenge of what you're undertaking with your own gender personally, what a rare and valuable opportunity to observe the cliques and roles around you with radically fresh eyes. It's fascinating." Zen looked back and forth between her Aunties, wondering—not for the first time—how two people who used words so differently could be married.

"I'm just glad our twiglet is snug home," said Aunt Phil. "While the spheres continue to roll in their orbits."

A long glance went between the two women, and Zen felt a sudden warmth as she watched them. She really did like them both. But oh, this new life, it was so completely new and strange. It still felt so close to impossible so much of the time.

Her phone chimed.

FOUR

Hello.

hello?
who is this?

Don't you know?

arli?

May I have my capital letter, please?

what?

My capital A.

Arli

Thank you!

really? u care about that?

Yes, I care about that.
I am a word geek.

jeezum, lookit u w all words spelled out
punctuation
nobody does that

I do.

You mean, like this?

Yes.

But it takes so long.

So?

And now that I've started,
I can't seem to stop.

It's like being bitten by a vampire.
Now you are a word geek too.

Curse you!

Avert!
I read that in a book once.

Me too! That one with the wizard school.

I mean, not That One
With The Wizard School.

Before that.

Yes, that one.

You still there?

Yes, I'm still here. :-)

Please don't do that.

Do what?

The smiley face thing.
Emoticons.

Why not?

They're dumb. I hate them.

Judgmental much?

OK, fine. I'll put it this way:
Words can always say it better.

That's what I believe, anyway.

OK, then, how about if I spell it out?
Smiley face.

All right, I'll allow it.

Thank you.
Any other rules about texting with you?

While we're on the subject,
Your Royal Texting Highness?

scratches head
I do like using asterisks to bracket actions.
"Star scratches head star."

nods thoughtfully

Like that?

Yes.

OK then.

OK.
And:
So?

So, what?

So, aren't you going to ask me?

I already did, remember?

That was before.

Aren't you going to ask me again?

rolls eyes

What if I don't?

Totally your choice.
But then you'll never know.

I could find out another way.

Oh yeah?

Yeah. If I wanted.

Like how?

Um, how about school records?

What are you, some kind
of Hacker Genius?

Maybe I am.

Wow face. Now I am impressed.

Are you still there?

rolls eyes again
OK, fine. What is your full name?

I thought you'd never ask.
Starling Kedum.

Starling?

Yes.

What an odd name.

You're not wrong.
But that's what it is.

13 letters. With no repeats.

Yes.

Nice.

Thanks.

Um . . .

Um, what?

How do you get Arli from that?

Middle four letters.

Puzzled face.

I wanted a nickname. But Star is pretentious.

And Ling sounds like I'm pretending
to be Chinese. I am not Chinese.
So: Arli.

You give a lot of thought to nicknames.

Word geek.

You are a strange person.

Grinny face!
Thank you, I'll take that as a compliment.

FIVE

THE DAY HAVING gone so much better than she had expected, Zen found it almost easy to face the mirror when she brushed her teeth before bed. Not easy. Almost easy. Even when her confidence spiked high, facing her reflection was never simple. And confidence spikes could not be relied on. Life in girl mode had turned out to be way more of a roller-coaster ride than she had expected. Her mood swung constantly, wildly, and her confidence with it. Which meant that, approaching mirrors, she never knew what she was going to see. Always, there was some boy. Usually a lot. The worst times, nothing but. Only once or twice had there been a heart-hammering moment of maybe beginning to see only girl. Even those moments were fraught, though. She yearned for them so much, and they never lasted more than a second. No way to hold on to the seeing. So fragile and elusive, it was.

She rinsed and spat, then raised her head and made herself look at her face. She tugged at her hair, wishing it were longer. She tried a kissy mouth. She twiddled the starter-studs in her ears, longing for the day when she could wear her first real earrings. She held her head at different angles and pulled with her fingers to bring out the shapes of the bones and cartilage under the flesh.

The other thing that made mirrors challenging was simply the passage of time. She lived in terror of the changes puberty would bring. The heavier, thicker facial bones. The beginning of an Adam's apple. The first dark hairs sprouting on her upper lip. Body hair. Bulking muscles. The first voice break. Other, more awful changes further down. Thank God, none of them had begun yet. She had been lucky so far, but it couldn't last.

It had taken the whole summer to work up to this day. In June there had been the first trip outside in girl mode, after nightfall along the quiet streets of their neighborhood, in an agony of trepidation, with Aunt Lucy there to hide behind when the one or two people they met walked past. Then the second, trembling and bold, in the middle of the afternoon down Congress Street, the busy main drag through Portland center. Then several more forays after that. All had been completely without incident—not even a single double take—and at last she had begun at least to hope, if not to believe or trust, that other people might really be seeing her as the girl she knew she was.

So: Try again tomorrow? It was going to be a constant question, fresh each day. Day at a time, Aunt Phil had said once, and inside, Zen had laughed bitterly. Day at a time! What luxury! Try hour at a time. Minute. Second, sometimes.

Today had been a bewildering, fear-drenched ordeal.

But, there had been good moments.

So, yeah, maybe, try again tomorrow. Final call in the morning.

Before sleep, Zen said her prayers. She had stopped actually kneeling by the bed, but it still felt good to close her eyes and direct her mind out and up, the way she had been taught. The way she had been doing for as long as she could remember.

Hello, God.

Thank you for me not dying today. Even though I felt like I was going to. And thank you for no one seeing that I have this stupid boy body. Thank you for getting to meet Arli and Dyna and Clem. Thank you for Aunt Lucy and Aunt Phil. Bless them. Bless them all. Please.

What am I doing? How can I even imagine this will ever work? But don't get me wrong, God, I'm so grateful to be trying. I lived a day as a girl today. As who I really am. In school. Thank you for that, from the bottom of my heart, of my soul. Thank you.

And bless everyone back home, too. Even though.

Please, God, give me the strength to do it again tomorrow. Thank you and amen.

SIX

THE PROBLEM WITH being so self-conscious on day one that you can't even hear words: day two is not too early to have missed something important. As soon as the first-period bell had rung, Mr. Walker asked everyone to take out their rubrics. Zen watched in blooming panic as the other students around her extracted a stapled packet from notebooks and backpacks. What rubric? What even was a rubric? "Did everyone have a chance to look through this?" Mr. Walker asked. A murmur of yesses. They had all done the homework Zen hadn't even known existed. Her face burned. "Any questions?"

Hands went up. Zen felt a touch on her arm and jumped. She turned and looked. The person who had touched her was a girl with long blond hair and sympathetic eyes. "Did you forget yours?"

"What?"

"Your rubric—did you forget it?"

"Um . . . yeah."

"You can share with me if you want."

Zen scanned the girl's face again and saw only kindness. "Thanks." They scooched their desks closer together, and, by craning, Zen was able to follow along. Whispering thanks and introductions, she found out the girl's name: Melissa.

When class ended, Zen lingered at her desk, summoning nerve. Mr. Walker had a natural kid-like enthusiasm about everything, and he just let it shine out, like, I don't care if you judge me for being such a geek, because I am. Even so, it was a challenge to approach him. She pulled her phone out and checked her dim reflection in the dark screen. She tugged down on a lock of hair by her ear. She walked up to the desk.

"Hey there," said Mr. Walker. "It's Zenobia, right?"

"Yes, sir." A beat. "My nickname is Zen."

"Okay, Zen, great. Welcome to Monarch Middle. You're new, right?"

"Yes, sir."

"Cool." Another beat. "So, what's up, Zen?"

"Um, yes, I'm sorry, I seem to have missed getting one of those rubric things yesterday."

"Is that all? No problem. I've got plenty more." He reached for his briefcase and pulled it up onto his desk, but then his gaze went out over Zen's shoulder. "Hey, Robert!" he said.

Zen turned and looked. A tall dark-haired boy was standing with one foot already out the door, looking back. "Yes, Mr. Walker?" the boy said.

"Do you have a second? I have a problem with my laptop,

and I know you know stuff about that. Could I get the benefit of your expertise?"

The boy's cheeks turned pink. "Sure," he said, coming back into the room.

Mr. Walker extracted a rubric from his briefcase and handed it to Zen distractedly as he moved around his desk, answering her "thank you" with a nod. He sat down at his laptop. Robert came over to where he could see the screen. Zen felt dismissed, but couldn't quite bring herself to leave. The old pull. Her jam.

Mr. Walker said, "Okay, see, when I sign on . . . Hold on, I'll restart. It happens every time. Okay, here we go. Startup screen . . . dum de dum . . . and there, did you see that? That little window that popped up for a second?"

"Yes, I saw," said the boy.

Zen shifted so she could see the screen, too.

"That never used to be there before," said the teacher. "And it feels like the machine has been running slower, too, for the last little while. And sometimes when I type, the letters don't appear for a second, and then they all burst out in a bunch."

Robert said, "When's the last time you defragged your disk?"

Zen shook her head. Her fingers itched to get at the keyboard.

Mr. Walker said, "I've never done that, as far as I know. I don't even know what it means."

Zen tuned out as Robert talked about how data gets

stored on hard drives. She stared at the laptop, all her alarm bells jangling. It had that dark-side feel. Robert finished what he was saying and left, hurrying to his next class.

Coming into this new school and this new life, Zen had made a rule for herself: don't get noticed. She couldn't help it, though. Robert's advice was wrong, and Mr. Walker was such a nice teacher, and anyway, she hated not saying what she knew. "Um . . ."

"Oh, Zen! You're still here. What's up?"

"I don't think defragging is going to help you."

"No?"

"No, sir. I think something else is causing the problem you're having."

"You know something about computers." It was nice the way he said it—an observation, not a question.

"Yes, I do. Do you mind if I look?"

"Well, the thing is, I have another class this period." Kids were already filling up the desks.

"Just a quick check. One thing."

"Okay, I guess so. Be my guest."

Zen sat down in front of the keyboard. As always at the gateway to Cyberlandium, her mind immediately switched to laser-concentration mode. She brought up the registry and scanned it. Yep, telltale signs. She summoned the list of running processes and saw a string of characters she knew. She began shutting down the computer.

"Wait, what?" said the teacher.

"Mr. Walker," said Zen, forgetting to feel self-conscious at all. In her element. "You have malware on your computer. A keylogger. Someone is capturing all your keystrokes and sending them somewhere."

"You could tell that in one minute?"

"Yes, sir. It's easy to find if you know what to look for."

"And how did you know—" The bell rang. Mr. Walker's face shifted. "All right, then, thank you, Zen," he said. "What should I do?"

"Um, the thing is, I'm late for my next class."

Mr. Walker tore a sheet off a notepad and scribbled something on it. "Right, of course," he said, handing her the paper. "Give this to your next teacher."

"And don't turn your computer on again until you know what to do," Zen said.

"But my lesson plan . . . all right."

"Okay. Thank you for this." Holding up the note.

"Thank you, Zen. Seriously, thank you."

"You're welcome, sir."

In the hall, bustling to second period, she peeked at the note. "Please excuse Zen's lateness," it read. "She was rescuing me from a Key Logger. Girl's got chops." Zen blushed again, this time from pleasure. So nice to have one's talent recognized, even for such a simple and easy thing.

SEVEN

ENTERING THE CAFETERIA, Zen was relieved to see the same three people at the same table as yesterday. She started to weave her way toward them, but then saw a face pointed her way from another table. The girl from Mr. Walker's class, what was her name? Melissa. She was sitting with a couple of other clean-cut kids.

When their eyes met, Melissa did a wave that was clearly not just a greeting, but an invitation too. Zen did a lightning calculation, then smiled and waved back in a casual way that returned the greeting, but pretended she hadn't noticed the invitation part. Then she continued on her original course. It had been a near thing, getting to school this morning. Almost, she had felt too afraid. And she was farther along in the possibly-making-friends department with the orphan misfits. They felt safer.

Heys all around as she sat down, with an extra nod to

Arli, acknowledging their new text connection. Then the talk that had been going on resumed, and she realized it was a language lesson. Dyna was teaching Clem the names of colors in French. "*Vert*," Dyna said, pointing at the wall, which was green.

"Vair," Clem repeated.

"Good," said Dyna. "But the French R is different from how you say it here in America. You must make a sound in the back of your throat. Like, what do you call it when you put water in your mouth and . . ." She tipped her head back, made a noise.

"Gargle," said Arli.

"Yes, thank you, that. You must gargle the R."

"Vair-r-r," gargled Clem.

"Yes, that is good! Now: *Le mur est vert*. The wall is green."

Clem repeated the phrase, and Zen and Arli exchanged a glance. His accent sounded really good.

"Excellent!" said Dyna, smiling.

"Language *chima*," said Arli approvingly.

Clem said, "Language what now?"

"Chima," said Arli. "It's a word from the Nezel language. It's sort of like a cross between 'expert' and 'genius.' Or like 'geek.' I say I'm a word geek, but I could also say I'm a word chima."

"Nezel?" said Zen.

"Yeah. From Nezelia."

Zen squinched her face. "I've never heard of it."

"Lots of people haven't. It doesn't exist anymore. But my father's family came from there. It's my heritage."

"Cool," said Clem.

"That word you were saying made me think of it," said Arli. "'Veir' is a word in Nezel too."

Clem opened his mouth to ask another question, but Zen interrupted. She had just popped the top on another Aunt Phil plasticware tub and was making ick-face at its contents: a viscous green liquid full of what looked like tiny beads. "Ew," she said. "What is it?"

Once again three pairs of eyes examined her lunch. This time, though, no one had any sure answers. "Is it maybe a kind of soup?" Dyna ventured. Clem said, "It looks like pond scum." Zen tipped the tub and the green stuff oozed stickily up the side. Arli said, "Star fights back gag reflex star."

"Yeah, no kidding," said Zen.

Arli said, "May I taste it?"

"I guess? If you really want?"

Arli dipped a delicate pinky-tip. Tasted. Made a face. Delivered a verdict: "It tastes the way lawn-mowing smells. Like grass clippings chopped up in a blender."

Zen scowled and put the lid back on the container. Her eyes stung, and she shook her head, berating herself silently. Seriously? Gonna cry about a yucky lunch? But as the table-chat moved on to other topics, she had to keep her head down. The green goop came as yet another blunt reminder of how far she was from everything she had ever known in her life before.

The dry pita triangles that made up the rest of her lunch offered no comfort whatsoever.

INTERLUDE: SEEING ZEN

Aunt Phil

Chickadee flew right into our hearts, gotta say. She hadn't been here two weeks before Lu and I, we both just fell in love. Such a fierce bright morsel of humanity.

Terrible what she had to go through to get here, though. Such a shame. Out there in that trailer, and her dad going deep loopy on the Bible-thumping and such toward the end, I guess. No doubt he had his reasons—as many different paths through life as people walkin' 'em, and each one groovy in its way, I suppose. But all the same, keeping her locked down like that. It amounted to house arrest, it did. Child abuse, really. I mean, that's awful to say, but, look at it. Locked away. That's just wrong. And cruel. And . . . well, I can't say all the way down to the bottom how dark that feels to me.

But, Zen, our baby Zen, she has some fiber in her, know what I mean? To hold on to who she was and is through all of that, and come out still able to speak her truth on the other side. Never been a parent, but now I got a pretty good idea of what that pride feels like.

To look at a young one in your charge when they face the trouble of the world with such grace. And, gosh, look at me leaking around the eyes. Got me all emotional.

Anyway, we're just so pleased to have her in our lives. What a treasure, that girl. What a treasure.

EIGHT

THURSDAY AT LUNCH, Arli and Clem were talking on banana phones. They kept glancing at Zen and Dyna, seeking response to their brilliant fruit-based sketch comedy. The two girls looked back, unsmiling. "Nothing?" said Arli.

Dyna said, "Excuse me, please. I do not understand what you are doing."

"Being funny," said Clem. "Or trying, anyway."

Zen would have laughed if she hadn't been distracted. She was listening to the gamers two tables away. Of course she had already marked them. How could she not? The jargon. Easter egg. NPC. And that way of talking that never admits but is totally based on everyone caring who is better. From what she had been able to hear so far, they were all scrubs. No surprise there.

Arli said, "What is the smallest possible unit of humor? A giggle? How about . . . Wait, I've got it. A snark!"

Zen answered Arli's eager-for-a-laugh expression with a

movement of the head that said, I'm listening. Arli's forehead furrowed. To what? Zen pointed with head and eyes back over her shoulder. Arli glanced, made a face. Who cares about them?

Zen cared. Someone was describing a familiar-sounding gameplay moment, but she wasn't sure yet if it was what she thought it was. She risked a peek. The speaker had wire-frame glasses and a button-down shirt. The others listened intently. But then talking kid stopped talking, because someone else had arrived at the table. The boy from Mr. Walker's class. Robert.

"Hey, Chopper," someone said. Fists were bumped. Robert sat down and took over the story from Wire-Frame Glasses, and a word he said confirmed which gaming platform they were talking about. A word, it was fair to say, that nobody else in the whole school knew the meaning of better than Zen did. The whole state, for that matter. The whole country.

The word was *Lukematon*.

Only he was saying it wrong.

"It's the best platform in the world," Robert said. Okay, that much was true. "It's still pretty new, so it isn't all that big yet, but it's going to be huge." Also true. "It's named after the person who invented it." *Wrong.* Zen gripped the table. Arli, Clem, and Dyna were all staring at her. "He's a recluse, and he lives in a fortified compound in Montana." Repeating one of the rumors Zen knew was going around the boards. Her brows bunched heavy and low. She shifted to rise.

"What are you doing?" Clem whispered.

"Mister Thinks He Knows Everything over there doesn't know what he's talking about."

"So?" said Clem.

"Yeah, what's it to you?" said Arli.

"So, he's wrong."

"How do you know?" asked Clem.

"It would take a long time to explain, but I know."

Arli said, "Okay, fine. Let him be wrong."

"Why would I do that?"

"Because for a second it looked like you were going to go over and talk to him."

"I was. I am."

Clem said, "You don't want to do that."

"Why not?"

"Because he's a total dickwad, and he won't take kindly to being shown up by a girl."

Zen relaxed her frown long enough to give Clem a quick ghost of a smile—for the assumption of her skill, but especially for *girl*. "That's his problem."

"He'll make it your problem," said Clem.

Arli said, "Star draws finger across throat star. What were you, homeschooled?"

"Since you ask, yes."

That was good for a silence at the orphan misfit table. Robert could be heard spouting on. "It's hosted out of Finland because he doesn't want anyone to know where he is. The only thing anyone knows for sure is the name: Luke Maton."

This was more than Zen could bear. She bolted up and out of reach before Arli could restrain her. She strode to the gamer table. Robert cut off in the middle of a sentence. Zen found herself facing five or six pairs of unfriendly eyes. She didn't care. Her voice came out loud, with a touch of a shake in it. Someone not paying enough attention might have thought she was close to tears. That someone would have been wrong. "You have no idea what you're talking about."

Robert and his cronies sat unmoving. The situation was unprecedented. No one seemed sure what to do. At length Robert shook himself and said, "What? Who are you?"

"It's not Luke MATT-on. It's LUKE-eh-mah-tohn. One word, four syllables, accent on the first. And it's not a person's name."

"Who *are* you?" Conversations had fallen silent at other tables. A good part of the cafeteria watched and listened.

"And the creator doesn't live in Montana. Dot F I is for Finland—you got that part right at least—but it's not a routing. The creator lives there."

Robert had his hands open now, looking around, like, You all saw, I was just sitting here and this crazy girl came up and attacked me.

"LUKE-eh-mah-tohn," Zen repeated, voice still shaking. "Put it into any good translator. It's a Finnish word. It means 'countless.'" Then she stood there, breathing hard and staring at him.

Robert stared back. Other people stared too. Zen's gaze

wavered first. She looked around. So many eyes. Suddenly she quailed, turned, and scuttered back to Arli's table. A ripple of laughter followed her. One more quick glance. The gamers were chattering and scoffing, except for Wire-Frame Glasses, who was gaping.

"What got into you?" Arli asked, looking appalled.

Zen had no answer except hands up to hide her burning cheeks.

NINE

THERE WERE OTHER frictiony things with the Aunties besides weird lunch food. For example, it felt like they had company over practically every evening. The apartment was small. The room they had given Zen was right off the living room. There was no easy way to avoid hearing. And all of the Auntie-friends liked to talk, and some of them laughed really loudly. Zen felt bad that it bothered her, but it did. The noise pressed on her. After a while the walls started to loom in and her breath came short.

She didn't feel like she could complain, though. The Aunties had been so kind, making space for her in their previously child-free lives. She felt like she already owed them more than she could ever pay back.

Also, growing up in the family she had, she feared anger. Back home in Arizona, her father had set the tone. Life had consisted of long, simmering silences punctuated by sudden explosions. She had hated it . . . even though she had also participated in it herself. Unable to avoid picking up the routine, immersed in it as she was. And it did express a never-tamed thing inside her. Like today in the cafeteria. When the rage welled up, she felt like she had no choice except to surrender and let it carry her where it would.

To be fair, neither of the Aunties had ever blown up at her. Zen kept getting drawn back to Aunt Phil's eyes. She had been unable to find any anger in them. But she didn't feel ready to trust that yet. As for Aunt Lucy, she was harder to read. She had an edge to her, for sure. And she was Zen's father's sister. They had grown up in the same family. She seemed like she could explode too, in the right circumstances.

Thank God, then, for Cyberlandium. The place she had discovered her natural genius. The place she had still been able to be someone when she had not been allowed to be someone in the actual world.

In her room, homework done for the evening, Zen sat down in front of her laptop, put headphones on to shut out the racket of Auntie-friends over for dinner, and brought up a stream of vintage country. Pining for the old days, even though they sucked so bad. She opened the Lukematon portal. The confrontation with Robert had awakened a desire to walk the secret tunnels once again. Before she could sign in, though, a chat window popped up. Arli.

Zen sat back for a second. Tammy Wynette twanged in her ears. Did she want to engage? Yeah, okay, sure. Lukematon could wait.

I repeat: What got into you?

You again.

Well, hello to you too.

Neener neener.

What are you, five years old?

Of course not.

Well, act your age.

Jeezum, you're bossy.

nods
shrugs
I repeat: I repeat: What got into you?

You think that's cute.
But it's not.

And don't even think of doing three.

Fine.
But you should know, I don't erase half-typed texts for just anyone. Why so crabby?

Are you there?

Yes

Uh-oh, your punctuation is disappearing. This is serious.

You are so annoying.

Thank you. I'll take that as a compliment. And I really do want to know.

Want to know what?

What got into you.

He just thinks he's so smart, is all. But he doesn't have a clue.

So?

It just makes me mad.

Why?

I can't explain. It just does.

All right, let me ask you this instead: How come you know so much about Lukematon?

Long story.

I love long stories.

Also, none of your business.

Wow, you really are crabby, aren't you?

So what if I am?

Good thing I'm so unrufflable.

I don't think that's a word.

OK, then, how about equanimitous?

I don't think that's a word either.

It is now.

I have to go.

Was it something I said?

No. Aunt Phil just called dinner.

Don't you mean Uncle Phil?

Now that you mention it, sort of.

Big-eyes face.
I'd like to meet this rentsib.

Rentsib?

You totally made that up.

Yes, I did.

What does it mean?

Parent Sibling.
It's a way to say aunt or uncle without gender.

Oh. Cool.

I really do have to go now.

OK, bye.

But, thank you.

You're welcome.
Um, for what?

You were right, I was crabby.

But not so much now.

Smiley face.

Oh. OK, you're welcome. Smiley face.

See you later.

waves Bye for now.

TEN

SO FAR THERE had been only one shopping trip, made harder by the fact that neither of the Aunties wore girl clothes or cared about them. Also, Zen's experience to date had been based on wistful imagining rather than the actual buying and wearing of garments. As a result, it had been a stressful challenge coming up with even just three school outfits that were maybe okay. What they had ended up with: the blue dress; a pair of jeans—seriously girl jeans, no way to see them as boy jeans, which made Zen so happy; and a couple of tops to go with the jeans. Three outfits. Which meant that by Friday she had worn them all once, and had to start over. She could only pray that no one would notice.

It did help that the dress was her favorite, even if it was too big. With the jeans there was the problem of the stupid bulge to deal with. Plus she just liked how she felt wearing the dress. Now if she could just get shoes to match. But, step at a time.

Third period, instead of regular English class, there was

an assembly. When Zen got to the auditorium, the doors weren't open yet. Inside, the sound system made a screeching noise. Still setting up, sounded like. She got in line behind a group of four girls. In one quick glance before averting her eyes, Zen observed that they all had salon hair and new-looking, fashionable clothes with accessories.

The first "Hey" she didn't react to, thinking it couldn't be for her. But then the group in front of her turned as one. "Hey," said the same voice again, and she looked up. The four girls were all staring at her.

The speaker was a tall, thin girl with glossy auburn hair, expensive-looking clothes, and pretty, dangly earrings. "You're new, right?" said Auburn Hair. Her voice seemed familiar, though Zen couldn't think why. "What's your name?"

"Um . . . Zen."

"Zen?"

"It's short for Zenobia." Her voice had sunk to an abashed whisper. All the judgy eyes.

Auburn Hair leaned forward. "What did you say? Speak up!" One of the other girls giggled.

Zen managed a bit more volume. "It's short for Zenobia."

"Zenobia. Wow."

Zen went back to looking at the floor.

Auburn Hair spoke again. "Cute dress."

Zen made herself look up again. All four still staring. "Um . . . thanks?"

"Or it will be when you grow into it." Auburn Hair

pinched the shoulder seams of her own top, a light sweater that fit her perfectly, and pulled it up so that her head was poking halfway out of the neck hole. She pooched her lips out like she had no teeth, rolled her eyes, and said in a goofy voice, "It's the hillbilly look." The other three girls laughed. Auburn Hair patted her sweater back in place. Then she tapped one of her friends on the shoulder and made a gesture with her head. The friend raised the phone she was holding and snapped a picture. Auburn Hair made a sound like "hm" and turned back around. The other three girls did likewise. One of them whispered something, and they all laughed again.

Feeling confused and threatened, Zen turned her back to the group, and was startled to see a familiar face. Melissa, again. Kind Melissa with the rubric and the invite-wave that Zen had willfully misunderstood. Their eyes met just as someone crash-barred the auditorium doors open. The line began to shift.

Melissa did something with her face that wasn't quite a smile, but still seemed nice. "Hi," she said in her soft voice.

"Hi," said Zen. Melissa, she noted, was wearing a little gold cross on a chain around her neck.

It was their turn to file forward. Melissa fell into step beside her, and together they turned into a row near the back. They sat down together. Zen felt tongue-tied, but Melissa didn't seem to mind. After a stretch of companionable sitting, Melissa said, "You shouldn't have let her do that."

Who? Do what? Zen still couldn't speak, but apparently her look managed to ask these questions, because Melissa said, "Olive. Natalie's friend. You shouldn't have let her take your picture."

Pure puzzlement at last made speech possible. "Why not?"

The answering frown said, Duh, isn't it obvious? "Haven't you ever seen *Mean Girls?*"

"No. What is it?"

"A movie. How can you not know that?"

Zen didn't answer.

"Were you homeschooled or something?"

"For a while. Why do people keep asking me that?"

Melissa was back to her first thought. "Well, anyway, pictures and stuff. Nothing good can come from that. Natalie Davenport isn't good for anyone but herself."

Brain click. "Natalie," Zen whispered. The girl in the bathroom on the first day, talking about corn husk hair. That was why her voice had been familiar. But the lights had gone down. It was time for the program.

While the motivational speaker spoke motivationally, Zen and Melissa exchanged looks and smiles a few times. Friendly, was how it felt.

INTERLUDE: SEEING ZEN

Natalie

The new girl? Yeah, I've seen her. Of course I've seen her. She was behind me in line at assembly. She's, like, a freaky homeschool doofus, you know? Or something? Looks like she just started wearing clothes yesterday. Like she doesn't even know what a dress is. What did she do, grow up in a cult? Where they had to wear, I don't know, like, overalls or something? Overalls and nothing else?

Oh, and Robert, you know Robert? Robert hangs out with some of the same people I do, and I heard him say she's, like, a cyber-expert freak or something. Or at least she thinks she is. Showing off her NAW-ledge. I missed it, but everyone was talking about how she yelled at him in the caf. What was that about? What kind of girl cares about stuff like that?

Gamer geek girls are the worst. They are just the most pathetic. Hanging around the loser boys who play those games—well, not Robert, he's pretty cool, but most of them are fat ugly losers—listening to them talk and pretending to be impressed, just so maybe someone will notice them. Pathetic? No, not even a little bit. Psssh.

ELEVEN

THE ENCOUNTER WITH Natalie and her posse stuck in Zen's brain like a goat's head burr, spiked and galling. As the day went on, her mood blackened. By the time she got home she was fuming.

As she approached the driveway she saw Aunt Phil out working in the apartment house's little front yard. She longed to get inside, to escape into Cyberlandium. She had the right kind of rage going to maybe check in on an old exploit, or even start a new one. But there was no way to get by unseen.

"Well, hey, twiglet," said Aunt Phil. "How was school?"

"Okay. I guess."

"Okay? That sounds less than happy as can be."

"Oh, so there's a rule now? I have to be happy?"

Back home, such talk might have begun an escalation. Aunt Phil stayed calm. "No rules," she said. "Rules can be such a bummer, right?"

"I guess."

"And, hey, it's Friday. You survived your first week."

"I guess."

"Hum. Okay then, what's up? Something got you riled, cupcake?"

Zen's mouth worked. "I hate this dress!"

"Oh? Right on, right on."

"I hate all my clothes! You don't know anything about shopping!"

"That's true. You're right about that."

Zen scowled. Aunt Phil never said what Zen thought she was going to say. It flummoxed her utterly. She flailed her hands and said, "Oh, leave me alone. I'm going to my room."

"Door's open, turtledove." Zen turned away. "But, one other thing." Zen turned back unwillingly. "We're in for a treat. We're going to have company for dinner."

"Again?"

"Yes."

Even irate as she was, Zen could feel how ungrateful it would sound to complain, so she contented herself with snarling, "So?"

"So, I thought you might like to know. Sprink is a lovely human. I think you'll like him."

"I doubt it."

"Well, we'll see," said Aunt Phil serenely, and went back to pulling weeds.

Zen stomped inside, but she couldn't quite summon a

door slam anymore. Why did Aunt Phil have to be so nice? Ruining a perfectly good bad mood.

In her room she threw her pack on the bed, opened her laptop, and entered the portal of Cyberlandium. She felt the knot between her shoulder blades ease a bit. The comfort and safety of being online never changed. Her ultimate refuge. She checked her regulars. Well, look there: a couple of new Kimazui episodes had been posted. Exploits could wait. That would do fine.

It was true, what Aunt Phil had said. She had survived her first week. She deserved a treat. She leaned back in her chair, clicked, and was swept away into the shadow-play and girl-heroics of her favorite esoteric subs-not-dubs bootleg anime.

～～～～～～～

An hour or so later, as the second episode was ending, there was a knock on the bedroom door. Aunt Lucy stuck her head in. "Our dinner guest is arriving," she said. "Will you come out and help us greet him?"

"Yes, m— Okay, Aunt Lucy." Zen closed her computer and followed her aunt to the front hall.

Their visitor turned out to be a big bear-shaped human with short gray hair and a bristly face. Oddly, he had a butter-fly painted on one cheek.

"Sprinkles!" said Aunt Phil, giving him a hug.

"Hello, darling!" the man said.

"Hello, Brad," said Aunt Lucy. "Face painters at the farmer's market again today?"

"Why yes, how did you know?"

Aunt Lucy said, "Brad, I'd like to introduce you to my niece, Zenobia. She's living with us now."

Zen found herself face to face with a red-cheeked moon full of grin. "Well, isn't this delicious! How do you do?" the man said, holding out a huge hand.

Zen grasped three fingers and shook. "Very well, thank you, sir. I'm pleased to meet you," she said.

The grin got bigger, if that was possible, and the eyes sparkled. All the eyes, so different everywhere. "Oh my, how very polite," he said. "Not like these salty old women amongst whom you find yourself now, at all." Aunt Phil whacked his shoulder, and he guffawed. Then he said, "That's a wicked cute dress."

Surprised, Zen blushed. "Thank you, sir."

"Honey, you're sweet," he said. "But please, don't call me 'sir.' I get more than enough of that at work."

Zen blushed again and dropped her eyes.

"We had to do some shopping when Zen first arrived," said Aunt Phil. "Her old wardrobe . . . got lost in translation." Zen glanced at Aunt Phil's face and felt a sudden rush of gratitude. Such care being taken. It made her feel . . . safe? A word she was so unused to using, she couldn't feel sure. Protected? Something.

"It was a little tricky, though," said Aunt Lucy. "We had trouble settling on more than a couple of outfits."

"Well, that will never do," said Sprinkles-Brad, looking

at Zen. "Bare minimum, girl's gotta have at least two weeks without repeating, am I right?"

Yes, that sounded exactly right, actually, now that he mentioned it. Zen nodded.

"The thing is," said Aunt Lucy, "neither of us actually knows all that much about—"

"Say no more! Gotcha covered!" Then, to Zen, "So how about it, girlfriend? Wanna go shopping?"

Zen flopped her mouth, then managed to stutter, "But . . . d-dinner . . ."

All three adults burst out laughing. Not mocking, though. Warm.

"Not this very instant, ducks," said their guest. The laughter coasted down. "Seriously, though," he went on, "I'd be happy to help."

Aunt Lucy said, "But not your usual—"

"No, of course not. Schoolgirl outfits. Prim, but also stylish, but also proper, but also fabulous. I know the exact sort of thing."

"That would be a great help," said Aunt Lucy.

Aunt Phil winked at Zen. "You've got all sorts of aunts and uncles now," she said. "Perhaps you didn't realize."

"Sure!" said their visitor. "The village it takes! You can call me Uncle Sprink if you like. Way better than sir." He didn't wait for a response to this, rooting instead in the depths of the canvas tote he held. "Anyway," he said, "that one stand I like had

squash so cheap it was practically free, so I brought you some."
He pulled lumpy vegetables out of the bag and handed them to
Aunt Phil, and the conversation moved on to local food.

At dinner Zen kept mum and listened. These people
were so nice, but they were so strange, too. What kind of a
name was Sprink? And Zen knew the words her father would
have used for this man—hard, wounding words, based just on
the lilt in his voice, the way he talked with his hands. Having
grown up around them, it was hard to keep those words from
popping up in her own mind too. Even though she knew that
her father would have had words just as hard for her. Not just
would have had. Had had. Had yelled.

As she helped clear the table after the meal, she experi-
mented with trying to begin to trust this tentative new sense
of security she seemed to be feeling. Each time she approached
it, all the old fears still welled up, instinctive and powerful.
Maybe with more practice, though, she could get past the fear.
Maybe someday soon she could begin to lower her guard at
least a little bit.

TWELVE

PERHAPS IT WAS just the roller coaster, or perhaps it was because, without quite realizing it, she had spent the whole first week braced for disaster, or perhaps both, but whatever the reason: Saturday morning when Zen got up, rather late, and stumbled bleary-headed into the bathroom, she looked in the mirror and saw nothing but boy. She recoiled and covered her eyes with her hands. She peeked again. Still, boy was all she could see. Her mood, already shaky, plummeted. This was insane. How could she possibly continue to pretend that the world might accept her? She began to shake, and from deep down a long wail rose up, unstoppable. Release of tension, the needle-sharp stab of hope, renewed spike of fear, all in combination maybe, came bursting out of her in a storm of tears.

Concerned Aunties came hurrying. She had no words, could not explain. They put her back to bed. When the weeping finally tapered, she drifted back into sleep, then woke again feeling drained and bleak. She lay for a long time staring at the ceiling. Aunties came and asked questions. She answered with monosyllables, grunts, silence. They went away again. She dozed some more, then managed to drag herself out of bed long enough to fetch her laptop. Kimazui: the ultimate comfort. The outfits. The outrageous anime hair. The kick-ass girls saving the world, routinely, from a new and different evil each week. It soothed her turbulent mind and salved her aching heart. Slowly the day passed.

As evening came on she began to feel lighter. She emerged from her room to find the Aunties preparing to go out. Aunt Lucy looked at her with a line between her eyes and asked, "Do we need to get you a babysitter?"

"She'll be all right," Aunt Phil said to her wife. "She's a smart and independent young human." Then, to Zen: "Am I right?"

Sometimes the Aunties talked like she was a little kid, which was infuriating. Other times, though, they acted like she was already an adult. As she had on other occasions, Zen jumped at the chance to claim more autonomy. "Yes, thanks, you're right. I'm fine by myself."

"Are you sure?" said Aunt Lucy. "We could find someone."

"I'm fine, thank you. So much better than this morning."

"Well then, as you like," said Aunt Lucy, and Aunt Phil added, "Right on." The Aunties gathered the food they were taking, put on shoes, and were gone.

Beyond just feeling comfortable alone, Zen loved the

moment when a door closed and she had a house to herself. She stood still, savoring the fading echoes. Not just sound echoes. People echoes. Humans took up so much space, and it was always so nice to feel the space springing back when they went away.

Her mood was shifting yet again. The roller coaster, swooping on into the next curve. She felt herself becoming hyper-alert. The ire was coming back too, like a turbine spinning up. She headed for her room.

Once aboard in Cyberlandium she sat drumming her fingers and staring daggers at the blinking cursor. She felt the need to visit righteous wrath on someone. The hot sweet fury. That pent-up thing. Her fingers hovered, on the edge of typing an address that would lead to a portal that would ask for an old black hat name . . . but then her hands dropped again. No, not quite that.

What about Lukematon, then? She had never ended up getting there the other evening. Yes, that would do very well.

She signed in, loaded one of her arsenal of warrior woman avatars, and entered one of the many game environments she routinely visited. Didn't matter which one—the secret doors were everywhere, once you knew how to find them. Next she teleported to a saved location out in the remote reaches of empty wilderness, far from all other players. On arrival she did a quick scan to confirm that she was alone and unobserved. Then she took from her virtual satchel a key.

This key was a strange and precious treasure, for it

unlocked the maintenance tunnels that ran under all the gaming platform's worlds. Actual virtual tunnels. Whoever had designed Lukematon had a whimsical sense of humor, giving admin space such atmospheric trappings. The key was the prize from what had been without doubt the toughest and finest hack of her career.

Zen ducked behind a certain tree. There was an iron ring in the grass near the trunk. She pulled on it and a trapdoor opened, draggling sod. Underneath was a thing like a man-hole cover—lower res than the gameplay, pixels plainly visible. That meant she was on her way inside. About to walk the secret corridors once again. She put the virtual key in the virtual keyhole and hauled the manhole cover open. She climbed down the cartoony steps into the gloom and pulled the cover shut again above her.

The tunnel had train tracks down the middle and was lit by the same naked-glare lightbulb over and over. She walked a path she knew, headed for a control hub. Scattered around the tunnel system were stations where a savvy person could work out how to do all sorts of things. One thing she had figured out so far: how to access lists of all the user IDs of players currently playing.

What had that insufferable Robert's friends called him? Chopper. Zen made a contemptuous sound. Screen name. Had to be.

In the control room she pulled down the virtual logbook and leafed through to the Cs. And there it was. Well, not exactly. But what were the chances Chopper789 was anyone else? And anyway, it didn't matter. Cyberlandium was a cruel place. A place of random Justice. And sometimes, when the mood was on her, Zen felt herself to be the Angel of Justice.

She entered invisibly into the game realm in which Chopper789 was playing. Sword and sorcery, what a shock. Another contemptuous sound. She examined the contents of his satchel. A Vorpal Sword? No way he had acquired that through straight gameplay. Bought it, probably. It would do for a start.

Zen practiced her art.

THIRTEEN

ON MONDAY, HAVING emerged the victor in a weekend wrangle about buying versus packing lunch, Zen halted on a patch of floor by the food court exit, where decades of pausing feet had worn through the tiles. The orphan misfit table had strangers sitting at it. What? Where was everyone? She scanned the room. No Arli, no Clem. There was Dyna, but she was sitting with other black kids, and Zen didn't feel up to trying to make a comfortable entrance at that table. So, where was she going to sit now?

What decided her was curiosity about whether she had guessed right about the identity of Chopper789. She swept her eyes past the gamer table. Robert was not there. Wire-Frame Glasses was, though, and, disconcertingly, seemed to be looking back at her. Or maybe not—his gaze skittered away. Zen shook the moment off. Robert had shown up late before, so maybe he would again.

She headed for a table one leapfrog away from the gamers.

Only one other person was sitting there: a shy-looking boy of, apparently, Asian descent. He sat at the very corner, folded into himself. Without asking, Zen sat down at the diagonally opposite corner. The boy kept his eyes down. He looked vaguely familiar. Was he maybe in Mr. Walker's class? Zen couldn't remember for sure.

She was halfway through her delightfully not green goop burger when Robert exited the food court. And, a couple of steps behind him, Melissa, who saw her looking and took it as an invitation. She came over and put her tray on the table. Robert meanwhile peeled off to the gamers, who welcomed him loudly. Zen answered Melissa's greeting with a distracted non-word. But Robert didn't immediately start talking about Lukematon, so after a bit she was able to connect with what was happening at her own table.

Which was Melissa trying to engage with the shy boy. "Hi," she had just said.

"Hi," the kid answered, not much above a whisper.

"I've seen you around, haven't I? Don't we have English together?"

"I don't know? Maybe?"

"What's your name?"

"Elijah."

Zen flashed back to the first day with Arli and said, "No way! What's your last name?"

The boy flinched. "My last name?"

"Yes."

"Um . . . Tuck."

"So how do you spell your whole name?"

Elijah Tuck spelled his name.

"Ten letters and no repeats," said Zen.

Melissa and Elijah both goggled at her. "What . . . ?" said Melissa. Looking distressed, Elijah picked up his tray and left.

"You scared him away," said Melissa.

"I don't see how."

"It was weird, what you said. What were you talking about?"

"The letters of his name being all different from each other. It's a thing Arli cares about—you know Arli, right? So now I've started noticing it too. That's all."

"Arli is weird."

"I think Arli's response to that might be, 'You're not wrong.'"

Melissa shrugged and started eating mac and cheese. Zen picked up her burger again, then froze. Someone had just said the word *dragon*. She did her best to turn her whole back into a giant ear. It was Robert speaking. Melissa took a breath to say something, and Zen whispered, "Shh! I'm listening."

"To what?"

"Just shh, please? Okay?"

Melissa looked annoyed, but stayed quiet. Robert was saying, ". . . the strangest thing. My sword was gone."

Zen made a silent face of fierce joy. Yes! It had been him.

"And then this dragon appeared. And all I had was this

stupid wooden stick that somehow my sword had turned into."

"Dude, no way," someone said.

"But that's not the strangest thing," Robert went on. His voice was shaking a little. Zen cupped a hand over her mouth. "So this dragon, I've seen screenshots, it's, like, the big payoff boss dragon, right? From the very highest level, end of the quest. And you have to have all this flame protection built up to face it, which I didn't have, so I figured I was toast. But then it opened its mouth, and what do you think came out?"

"Fire!" said one voice. "What?" said a couple of others.

"Not fire." A pause, but not for dramatic effect. From his breathing, he was seriously upset. "Mice."

There was a silence. "Say what now?" said a voice.

"Mice. The dragon opened its mouth, and this, like, waterfall of mice came out onto me. I was completely buried in falling mice."

Zen had both hands over her mouth now and was making little crying noises.

"Are you okay?" asked Melissa.

Zen nodded. She closed her eyes and concentrated on breathing through her nose. She absolutely positively could not laugh.

"What's the matter? Do you have a toothache?"

It was as good an explanation as any. She nodded again. "I get that too," Melissa said. "When I eat cold things, sometimes. Ice cream. Stuff like that."

Zen nodded one more time, feeling her breathing settle back toward normal. At the gamer table, someone said, "Did you get your sword back?"

"Yeah," Robert said. "I logged out and logged back in again, and everything was back to normal." True. The mouse-breathing dragon accomplished, Zen had felt satisfied with the exploit and relented. It had been so much fun, though. No denying the old thrill.

Melissa's mind had gone on to something else. "May I ask you something?" she said.

Zen couldn't read Melissa's expression. Had she been found out? Was she about to be outed? Adrenaline surge. Not trusting speech, she did her best to prepare herself.

"Um . . . would you like to come over to my house this weekend?"

There was nothing in Melissa's face but kindness, with a touch of bashful. False alarm. Zen took a moment to ride down the shakes. This girl. She was just really nice. And she wanted to be friends. "Okay," she said.

"We do games sometimes on Sunday afternoon."

"Okay."

"Me and my family."

Zen remembered manners. "Thank you very much for the invitation. I would be honored to be your guest."

Melissa smiled. She had a pretty smile, in a wholesome toothpaste-ad sort of way. "Okay, good," she said.

FOURTEEN

Where were you today?

Oh, hello.

Hello. Where were you?

I'm doing all right. Thanks for asking.

Are you being sarcastic?

rolls eyes What do you think?

Um, are you sick?

I wasn't feeling well.

Oh. OK, I'm sorry.

I didn't realize.

And I didn't mean to sound cross.

"Cross." What a great word.

Are you there?

My mom used to say it.

You were quiet for a minute. Your mom?

Are you there?

She passed away a long time ago.
When I was little.

Tear on cheek face. I'm sorry to hear that.
I didn't mean to bring up a painful subject.

sighs It's OK.

But you remember her saying "cross."

Yes.

So it can't have been when you were a baby.

No. I was five.

What about the rest of your family?
If that's not also a painful subject.

Well, I don't really have one.
Anymore.

?

I've never seen you not use words.

Because I'm astonished.
How can you not have a family?

Not no family.
There's Aunt Lucy, of course.
And Grandma Gail.

But, um, let's just say, we're not all that close.

No siblings?

No. Only child.

What about your other parent?

My dad? He died. Too.

Jesus!

My mom wouldn't have liked that.

Liked what?

Taking the Lord's name in vain like that.

She was religious?

Yes. Very. My dad too.
Especially after my mom died.

What happened to him?
If you don't mind me asking.

I don't mean to pry, but I am curious.

Hunting accident.

J . . . Um, Oh My Goodness! When?

In April.

April of this year?

Yes.

Oh.
My.
Goodness.
Crying face.
I'm so sorry.

Are you there?

Yes, I'm here. Thinking.

Because, I've never cried.
Of course I miss him.

And of course it's terrible what happened.
And I did love him.

I mean, you have to love your parents, right?
But, he was so mean to me, and he didn't

He didn't . . . what?

Something I can't say.
But it was so hard. Living with him.

OK. And now you live with your aunt?

My two aunts. Aunt Lucy and Aunt Phil.

I have GOT to meet these people.

Puzzled face. Why?

Because they sound so cool.
Are they married?

Yes.

You have to invite me over.

Jeezum, you're bossy.

I'm telling! You took the Lord's name in vain!

"Jeezum" doesn't count.

Yes, it does. It has "Jeez" in it.

No, trust me, it doesn't. My mom said so.

That's where I got it from.

OK, if you say so.
So?

So, what?

So, are you going to invite me over?

Why don't you invite ME over?
That would be the polite thing to do.

puts hands on hips
Well, excuse me, Miss Manners.

You don't have to be sarcastic.

I care about that stuff. I was raised that way.

What way?

The polite way.

Oh. Well, that's fine then.
But I can't ask you over.

Why not?

I mean, it's not that I can't, in the sense
that it's impossible. It's just complicated.

Complicated how?

Could you just take my word for it, please?

OK.

Thank you.
So . . .

So what.

So, if you're taking my word for it, then there's
only one other way for us to get together.

rolls eyes OK, fine.

Would you like to come over sometime?

Yes, thank you, I would.

I mean, I have to ask.
But I think they'll say yes.

Thumbs-up hand.

And I hope you're feeling better.

Yes, I am, thanks.

OK. Talk to you soon.
Bye for now.

Bye for now.

FIFTEEN

WEDNESDAY MORNING THE second week of school, Zen was sipping orange juice at the kitchen table and Aunt Phil was cooking a scramble at the stove when Aunt Lucy came in, holding her phone. "There's been an incident at Monarch Middle," she said. "I just got an email."

Aunt Phil turned, spatula in hand. "What happened?"

"It's from your principal, Zenobia," Aunt Lucy said. She put on a reading voice. "'Dear parents and guardians. Please be advised that early this morning the Monarch Middle School website was defaced. The perpetrator or perpetrators breached security and gained access by unknown means in order to post images disrespectful to people of the Muslim faith. As soon as the act was discovered, the images were removed.' Dah dah dah . . . 'We are treating this episode seriously'—well, I should certainly hope so—'and when we discover by whom this hateful act was perpetrated, that person or those persons will be prosecuted to the fullest extent of the law. Monarch Middle

School reaffirms its commitment to diversity and to celebrating the inherent worth and dignity of all of its students regardless of . . .' et cetera, et cetera."

"Well, that's just a shame," said Aunt Phil, shaking her head. She turned back to the sputtering eggs.

"It's an outrage, is what it is," said Aunt Lucy. "These times we live in. It never seems to end."

"Poor Dyna," Zen said. "I wonder if she knows yet."

"Who's Dyna?" asked Aunt Lucy.

"A friend of mine. She wears one of those head scarves . . . you know."

"You've made a Muslim friend? That's wonderful! How did you meet?"

"Um, could I tell you later? There's something I need to do." Professional curiosity, so to speak, definitely in play. "May I be excused?"

"Of course," said Aunt Lucy. "You don't have to ask."

Into her room to pull up the school's website. Yep, it was already fixed, just like the principal's email had said. The most recent news entry was for a date last week, so they had probably restored from the last backup. The site was primitive—common platform, stock design. Unlikely there was any extra security beyond the easily hackable default stuff. Her fingers itched to get at the server this ran from. Were there traces? How sophisticated had the attack been?

Aunt Phil called out that breakfast was ready, and Zen

reluctantly pulled herself away. She would ask Mr. Walker about it, though, for sure. Maybe they would let her help.

During breakfast Aunt Lucy said, "Zenobia, I wanted to mention, I looked into some of those treatment options we talked about." Zen held her breath, in instant suspense. This was the continuation of a discussion she could hardly believe was happening. As impossible as it seemed, after there having been no hope of any such thing for so long, the Aunties seemed willing to maybe help her with the medical part. Aunt Lucy went on: "I called the clinic in Boston, and I got us an appointment. They have a wait, I'm afraid, but we're on their calendar now. November."

The Aunties, never having been parents before, had been so clunky in some ways. The weird stuff in the fridge that did not look, smell, or taste like actual food. The raucous late nights. The casual conversations about subjects Zen had never heard discussed out loud before, that once or twice had caused her to flee to her room.

But there was no denying they had been wonderful in other ways. The whole girl project, front and center, obviously. Just rolling with that. Including the phone call Aunt Lucy had made in the last week of summer about PE, getting her out of that impossible puzzle with a made-up excuse.

And now an appointment with a gender doctor.

Zen had done some homework about that, despite the intense squirminess it brought on. *Dysphoria*, she had learned that squirminess was called—a name for the twisty, awful disconnect trans people could feel between body and brain. Oh, and let's not neglect to mention the powerful squidginess Zen also happened to feel about medical stuff, particularly anything that changed or invaded her body. Shots, for example. Nope nope nope. When she had been smaller, even haircuts had been difficult.

Still, pushing through the discomfort, she had been able to educate herself some about the treatments the people at this clinic might talk about. Hormone blockers. Well, that wasn't so bad. She could take a pill. Unless it was a shot. Squirm! And, later, things like surgery? Instant turbocharged shiver-willies. But then, on the other other hand, there was also the part where she wanted it with every atom of her being.

Both Aunties were looking at her, seeking response to the news. Laughing eyes and intense eyes. Zen knew she would cry if she spoke, but, manners. Her thank-you was no less sincere for being tearful. Then, overwhelmed by feels, she grabbed her pack and made a fast escape.

On her way to school, she did her best to force her mind away from the endless loops of desire and fear Aunt Lucy's news had started spinning. Gotta stay sane. Think about anything else. Think about the hack. That would do. She had a chance maybe to use her skills for good. Holding on to this thought like a life preserver, she made her way to Mr. Walker's room.

SIXTEEN

FIRST PERIOD BEGAN with announcements on the scratchy-sounding speaker in the corner of the ceiling, and that included Mr. Vann, the principal, telling again about the hack. People around the room exclaimed and made sad faces, but also someone snickered—one of the boys near the back. Mr. Walker looked up sharply, to see a row of carefully blank expressions. Robert's was among them. Zen, head low over her desk, peeked at him under the curve of her arm. Was he smirking?

During class, Melissa kept trying to catch her eye, and then held out a note. Zen felt both warm and annoyed. The attention was gratifying, of course, but things with this girl were happening faster than she wanted. It wouldn't do to just cut her off, though, so she waited until Mr. Walker was writing on the whiteboard to take the square of paper. She unfolded it and read, "Don't you think Robert is cute? He goes to my church." There was a smiley face and a heart.

Ugh. Really? Zen did her best to smile in response, though, because it was so clearly expected. The smile felt completely fake on her face. Melissa smiled back . . . and scribbled another note and held it out.

Zen really did not want to take this one. She shook her head minutely and made a little gesture toward the front of the room, pretending she was afraid of getting caught. Melissa's smiled snuffed out, and she withdrew the note with a wounded expression. Zen sighed and kept her eyes forward for the rest of class.

When the bell rang, Melissa was right there. "You didn't take my second note."

Zen had eyes on Mr. Walker. "I'm . . . I didn't . . . Sorry."

Melissa frowned for another second, but then shrugged. "Well, what it said was, let's sit together at lunch, okay?"

"Um . . ."

"What's the matter?"

Mr. Walker's period-two class was filling seats. "Um, I kinda already . . . I usually sit with Arli and those guys."

Melissa made a face. "What do you want to sit with those weirdos for?"

"I don't know. They're fun, I guess."

Melissa made a face. "Suit yourself," she said coldly. But then she switched back to a lighter tone. "So, did you get permission to come over?"

"I haven't asked yet. I will tonight." Zen took the extra

second to make eye contact and smile. "I really do want to come. It was nice of you to ask me."

"Okay. Wanna walk to our next classes together?"

"I gotta ask Mr. Walker something."

Melissa's face closed up again. Back and forth, back and forth. "Fine," she said, and turned away with a flip of the hair. Zen scowled. Girl stuff. Why did everything have to be so complicated? But her window was quickly closing. She went to Mr. Walker's desk.

"Hey, Zen," said Mr. Walker. "I wanted to let you know, I took my laptop to a friend of mine, and he said you were exactly right about that keylogger. He said he was impressed one of my students found it. So, thanks."

"You're welcome, sir." There was maybe a minute left, tops. "Mr. Walker, can I . . . Would it be okay if I . . ."

"What's up?"

"The website hack."

"Yes, what about it?"

"Well, you saw, I have skills. Maybe I could help figure out who did it."

Mr. Walker nodded. "It's interesting you should mention that, because, as it happens, I am one of the teachers responsible for the school website." Zen only barely stopped herself from rolling her eyes. "And I know you know things. But do you really think you could find out who it was?"

"Maybe? If I had access to the server?"

"Hm. I don't even know where that is."

"Or," she said, and this was the point she really wanted to make, "I could set up a tracker, so if the person comes back, we can snag an IP address." The bell rang.

"Hm," the teacher said again. "We both have our next classes. I will talk to the web committee and get back to you."

SEVENTEEN

WHEN ZEN EXITED the food court holding her tray, eyes. The first week it had been any eyes, all eyes. A general anxiety about being seen. Now it was eyes with meanings and agendas. Over there in that corner, Natalie and her posse, noticing her. Someone made a comment, and the table giggled. At the gamer table, Wire-Frame Glasses staring at her. Paul, his name was, Clem had said in answer to a carefully casual question. Farther around the room, Melissa at the clean-cut kids' table, giving her one flat look before pointedly looking away. And, the orphan misfits smiling hello. Except Dyna wasn't there. Zen wove her way over.

"Greetings, earthling," said Arli.

"Hey," said Clem.

Zen sat down. "Hi." She looked at the empty seat. "Where's Dyna?"

The question sucked away the table's mirth.

"What?" said Zen. "Is she okay?"

"As far as we know," said Arli.

"Her parents took her out of school," said Clem. "Because of the, you know . . . the thing that happened with the website. A couple other Muslim kids are out today too."

"Oh," said Zen. "Was it as bad as that? I mean, like, threats?"

"They got it down fast, but there are rumors," said Clem.

"What was actually posted?" asked Zen. "Do we know?"

Arli said, "I heard it was just derogatory."

Zen looked a comment: Well, now, that's some word you just used there.

Arli's look back said: Duh, word geek. Then, in a low voice after a glance around, "Grumpy Cat with, 'Muslims, go home,' is what I heard."

Clem leaned close and outright whispered: "I heard, a picture of a guy with a gun and, 'raghead hunting club.'"

"Jeezum."

"I know, right?" said Clem.

"That's just awful," Zen said, and the other two nodded.

In the silence that followed, Zen caught sight of that kid, what was his name? Elijah. The shy boy. He was making his way among the tables. Zen knew the shy playbook, and thought maybe he was angling accidentally-on-purpose toward them. And now he was slowing as he passed behind Arli and Clem. He gave one forlorn look. He wanted an invite.

Poor kid. She certainly knew how it felt. This was maybe going to be a little tricky, because the feel was that Arli was boss of the table. But, that look. "Hey," she said.

Clem and Arli turned to see who she was greeting. Elijah said something that might have been "Hi," if it had had any actual breath behind it.

"Do you want to join us?"

Arli gave her a hard glance. Yep, definite boss vibe. But then Arli's eyes softened. A nod. "Yeah, sit if you want." Then space was being made, and Elijah sat down.

Clem said, "Welcome to Arli's table of orphan misfits." Let the ritual commence.

Elijah looked alarmed. "Thank you?"

"My name is Clem."

Silence. Zen stepped in. "And I'm Zen."

"And I'm Arli," said Arli.

Yet more silence. Then, "My name is . . ."

As Zen was anticipating, Arli cut in. "Gizmo."

Elijah looked up full-face for the first time. "Excuse me, no?" he said. "My name is Elijah?"

"Do not question the Nickname Genius." But Arli's rhythm was off. The ritual was going bumpily.

Zen put out a placating hand. "It's a thing," she said. "We all have nicknames. Arli picks them."

Elijah did a sort of helpless face shrug. "Okay?" he said. Then, "What does Gizmo mean?"

Arli's eyes lit up. "It means thingamajig. Whatchama-callit. Doohickey. Thingamabob. Whatsit. Jobberdoo!"

"Synonym ecstasy," said Zen, and to her surprise, Arli burst out laughing. Clem followed. Clem had an incredibly goofy laugh, and after a couple of seconds Zen and Elijah couldn't help joining in.

As the laughter wound down, Zen said to Arli, "Gizmo? Where did you get that one?"

"Out of thin air. It came to me in the moment."

"So, not always a reason."

"You learn fast, grasshopper."

"Grasshopper?"

"If you don't know the reference, I'm not going to tell you."

The table had its mirth back, and lunch went by quickly. One bit of odd unpleasantness on the way out, though, as Zen and Arli passed the popular kids' table. Only Natalie and one friend were still there, sitting with their backs turned. As they passed, Natalie whispered, "Now," and both girls pinched their shoulder-seams and lifted their tops toward their ears. One of them made a sort of horking noise, and they both laughed. A little pit of pain opened up in Zen's stomach. She was wearing the dress again, just like Friday.

"What was that about?" Arli asked in the hall.

"I have no idea," Zen said stonily. So not wanting to explain. The promised clothes-shopping trip, if that was really going to happen, could not come fast enough.

INTERLUDE: SEEING ZEN

Paul

Her nickname is Zen, but her full name is Zenobia July. I found that out. I heard them talking about her in the office, and I remembered. She's about four feet eleven inches tall, which I know approximately because she was standing next to Walter Bowman in the hall for a minute between classes and they looked like they were exactly the same height, and then I stood next to Walter Bowman later in Mr. Ellison's class by the pencil sharpener and looked at where his head reached on the poster on the wall, and then I measured with my hand where my head reached on the poster, and it was about two inches higher than Walter Bowman's head, and I'm five feet one inch tall.

She knows a lot about games. I was at the table with Robert and Mike and those guys at lunch, and she came over and told us some stuff about Lukematon, which I only just learned about. Some of the guys didn't believe her, but I looked it up, and she was right, it's not Luke Maton, the person who made the platform, it's Lukematon, which means, just like she said, "countless" in the Finnish language. "Countless" because anyone who wants to, well, anyone who has earned enough in-game points anyway, can get access to some of the developer tools and start building their own game. You have to earn it, and it looks like no one has been able to find any cheats, and you only get a few points at a time, but in theory you could have any number of games on the site. So that's why "countless."

What does she look like? Well, um, she's . . . I don't know . . . I guess she has dark hair that it looks like she wants to grow out, because it's pretty short and sometimes she pulls at it like she wishes it reached down to her shoulders. And I guess her clothes are a little weird. I heard someone making fun of her clothes. But who cares about clothes, I mean, right?

Do I think she's pretty?

I dunno. Stop bugging me, okay?

EIGHTEEN

WALKING HOME FROM school, Zen pondered the puzzle of Melissa. She had been so thoughtful about the rubric, and she had been kind to Elijah, too, but there also seemed to be this complicated set of unwritten rules, and if Zen didn't say and do everything just right, Melissa's feelings got instantly hurt. It was baffling.

On the other hand, an invitation was an invitation, and Zen really did want to be friends. Melissa reminded her of girls she had known back home. She hadn't known them well— it was different when people saw you as a boy—but still, there was a familiarity there. The cross she wore. The politeness in the way she talked, that felt like Sunday at church. Being around Melissa raised an echo of an old feeling of belonging.

So, if Zen wanted to pursue the friendship, that meant she had to follow through on asking permission from the Aunties. One good time for such matters, she had figured out, was the moment that usually happened toward the end of dinner when Aunt Lucy started talking house business.

This particular evening, that moment came when they were halfway through dessert. Aunt Lucy put down her fork and announced that she had set it up with Brad—Uncle Sprink—to take a trip to the mall together on Friday night. Thank God! Zen took extra care with her thanks, wanting to make sure the Aunties understood how much it mattered to her. Then, while they were nodding and looking pleased, she cleared her throat and said, "Um, speaking of the weekend, I have a question."

"Yes?" said Aunt Lucy.

"I've gotten an invitation . . . a girl at school . . . she said, could I come over on Sunday? Get a ride and go? For a family game time they do?"

Aunt Lucy said, "Who is this girl?"

"Melissa Martin, her name is. She's in my social studies class." Silence. "She helped me with a homework thing. She's nice."

The Aunties exchanged a look. It was Aunt Phil who answered. "Sure, honeybunch," she said. "We'll be happy to drive you, and pick you up after." Aunt Lucy made a scoffing noise. "Well, what I should say is, your auntie Lucy will be happy to drive you. Me and cars, we don't get along real well."

Zen said, "Thank you."

"It's all right," said Aunt Lucy.

Aunt Phil said, "So you're making friends. Right on."

"Yes, m— Yes, thanks."

"Including that Muslim girl," said Aunt Lucy.

"Yes."

"Anyone else?" said Aunt Phil.

"Well, there's this kid named Arli."

"That's an unusual name."

"That's what I said too."

Aunt Phil laughed. "And what did Arli say in return?"

" 'You're not wrong.' "

Aunt Lucy snorted. "I like the sound of this person."

"Arli said that too!" said Zen. " 'I have to meet these peo-ple.' Meaning, you."

"Well, that's groovy," said Aunt Phil. "Maybe you could ask Arli over to play sometime."

Zen rolled her eyes. "We're not six years old, you know. We don't play."

"No?"

"So what do you do?" Aunt Lucy asked.

Zen thought for a second. "We hang out."

"Right on," said Aunt Phil. "Well, if you want to invite Arli to come hang out sometime, you can. Or to dinner. Or both. Feel free, pumpkin."

"Thank you," said Zen. She had been saving the Arli ask, not feeling sure how much she should try for at once. But, there, it had fallen into her lap. Arli would be happy. When she decided she was ready to issue the invitation. One friend visit at a time—that felt about right.

NINETEEN

FRIDAY NIGHT AT the mall, with Aunt Lucy in tow to wield the credit card, Uncle Sprink took charge. "All right, honey, talk to me," he said as they stood by the mall map. "What's your target look?" His eyes were alive with pleasure, and Zen all of a sudden felt a flower of happiness bloom in her chest. He was asking her what she wanted to wear. What girl clothes she wanted to wear. It was a lovely, lovely feeling.

Not that she had any clear idea how to answer. But it felt safe saying so. "I . . . don't know for sure?"

"No problem," said Uncle Sprink. "Let's see if we can narrow it down." He studied the mall map, then put his finger on one of the colored shapes. "This store, for instance," he said. "Baby punk. Tons of attitude. Black eyeliner. Too emo to ever smile."

"Um, no. I don't think that sounds right."

"Okay, then, let's see. Hm. No, too grown-up. No, also baby punk. Hm." He put his finger on another shape. "Okay, this one. Polite and formal, verging on prim. Tea with the queen. Very very too too."

Zen laughed. Warming to the task, she said, "No, not that either."

"Okay then, how about this one? Precociously sexualized, latest hot trends, don't-mess-with-me attitude, gonna take down the queen bee someday or die trying."

"Um . . . no, sorry? Not me either." Though she couldn't help thinking for a moment of Natalie.

"Maybe we're going about this the wrong way," he said. "How about this: What looks have you seen that you like? In movies or on the net or in the world?"

The answer was right there. "Kimazui."

"Beg pardon, sweetie?"

"Kimazui."

"What is that?"

"It's . . . it's my show. My favorite."

"And it has a look?"

"Yes."

"How would you describe it?"

"Well . . . it's Japanese, so you know, there's a thing with dresses with bows. But a little different, too. Not exactly like any other show."

Uncle Sprink pulled out his phone and did some fast thumb-typing. Then they were looking at stills together. "Ah," he said. "I'm with you now. Anime princess with a big dollop of cyberpunk. Very nice. It suits you well."

Glow glow glow. Who knew it could be so much fun talking about clothes? With a man who looked like a big friendly bear? Or anyone?

"Tricky," Uncle Sprink said. "No one store is going to have all of this. We're going to have to do some sleuthing."

What followed was a joyous whirlwind of dress-up play. At least, that was how it felt to Zen. Uncle Sprink was amazing. He bossed the salespeople around and whipped things off racks and held them up in front of Zen and frowned and put them back or smiled and added them to a growing cartload ranging from variations on the cyberpunk anime princess theme to things Zen would never have thought of, but was astonished to find she liked in the changing room mirror. Tangerine-colored capris. A knee-length T-shirty top with a huge flower on it. As well as other more regular girl clothes such as she had seen regular girls wearing at school. Some outfits she had to hastily take off again because she could see in the mirror that the stupid bulge would be a problem, but that always happened when she was alone, so the ick factor stayed manageable, and she felt safe enough to go on. Aunt Lucy brandished the card, and their collection of bags grew.

They had all agreed that they would try just one more store—shoes, oh joy!—when, coming around a corner, Zen found herself face to face with Dyna. There was a moment of fluster, and then the man who was clearly with her nudged Dyna a little behind him and stepped in front. Already launched into her greeting, Zen ended up delivering it mostly to him: "Hi?"

The man's eyes were on Uncle Sprink's face. His expression looked frightened, edging into hostile. Dyna said something to him in a language Zen didn't think was French. The man pushed her farther back behind him.

Aunt Lucy stepped forward. "Hello," she said. "It appears the girls know each other."

The man turned his wary gaze to her.

"My name is Lucille Jarecky," Aunt Lucy said. "And this is my friend Brad Haynes, and this is my niece, Zenobia."

Zen said, "I know Dyn— Chantal from school. We . . . we're friends."

The man's face unclenched a little. Dyna stepped around him, and he let her. "Hello, Zen," Dyna said.

"Hello." Zen made a pain face. "I'm sorry about what happened with the school website."

"It is not your fault."

"No, of course not." Pause. "But since here you are, I can tell you, I'm going to help figure out who did it."

The man said, "You are a friend of my daughter?" He had a heavy accent.

"Yes. My name is Zenobia July." She held out her hand. The man looked at it, and there was an awkward moment. Zen put her hand down again. The man did a little sort of bow-dip and said, "I am called Amadou Kasongo."

"Pleased to meet you," Zenobia said.

"I try to tell him," Dyna said. "Here in America, on the internet, always there are memes. And for the most part, they are empty. Not real danger. But he has fear."

Uncle Sprink said, "That's totally understandable."

Another silence, but with less tension. Almost friendly. Nonetheless, shopping called. "Okay, nice to see you, but we have to go," said Zen. Good-byes, and on to the shoe store.

In the car on the way home, Zen said, "Brad Haynes."

Uncle Sprink glanced back. "Yes?"

"So where does 'Sprink' come from?"

The two adults in the front seat exchanged a look.

"It's part of my drag name, honey," said Uncle Sprink. "The full name is Sprinkles La Fontaine."

"Oh," said Zen, and asked no more. She knew a little about drag from her web research. Drag was performance, the gender 101 sites said. As opposed to trans, which was about who you were. So Uncle Sprink was a drag performer. As he and Aunt Lucy continued to talk to each other, she studied the side of his face. He had a big head, not much hair at all, a big nose, big ears, stubbly cheeks. Try as she might, she couldn't see anything womanlike about him. She wondered if she would ever get to see him dressed up.

Uncle Sprink noticed her looking and gave her a smile and a wink. Zen smiled back. It went along with a sudden warm feeling in her chest. What did it matter, whether she could see woman in him at all? And what did it matter, the words her father would have had for him? It had been truly kind of him, taking her shopping. School next week was going to be so much easier because of it. She decided to like him until further notice.

TWENTY

THE ROUTE AUNT Lucy's phone chose to the Martins' house took them around a tree-lined bay and on into quiet suburban streets. Zen stared out the window at all the green. No place in Arizona was as green as this place. She still hadn't gotten used to it. Aunt Lucy drove intently, her mouth drawn down at the corners.

The Martins' house turned out to be a two-story place in a cul-de-sac, with a peaked roof and white siding, neat and prosperous-looking. Two cars stood in the driveway, and they both had fish emblems on them. One also had a church bumper sticker and a vanity plate: SOGR8FL. Aunt Lucy muttered something.

"I'm sorry?" said Zen.

"Nothing," said Aunt Lucy. "I guess I just didn't realize how far we were venturing into the Red State part of town." You could hear the capital letters in how she said it.

"Oh." Zen thought about her old family and their friends

back in Arizona. She wondered what Aunt Lucy would say if she knew that Zen still said her prayers before bed.

"No matter," said Aunt Lucy. "I'm sure they are perfectly decent people. But if you need to call, call."

"Okay, thanks."

Zen got out. The front door opened, and Melissa came out onto the porch. A woman with abundant curly red-blond hair came out too. They both had big smiles on their faces as they waved and called welcome. "Thank you for the ride," Zen said.

"I'll be back at five sharp to pick you up," said Aunt Lucy, looking impatient to be gone.

"Okay, thanks." Zen chunked the door shut and made her way up the walk.

Inside, Zen thought for a second that there was other company, but then she realized it was all one family: Mom, Dad, and five children. Melissa was second oldest. There were three younger ones clattering around, and older brother dude, who was in high school and who was tall and handsome. When he directed his distant boy gaze at her for a second and said hello, Zen felt a flippy sensation inside. He was *cute*. And he was gone, off into his room. Too mature for game day, apparently.

Then there was Mr. Martin, a polite man with a dress shirt and army-short haircut who said, "Welcome to our home, Zenobia," even as a couple of the smaller kids yanked him by the arms back toward the low table where he would be the grown-up in charge of crazy eights.

And, finally, Melissa's mom, the woman from the porch. Up close, Mrs. Martin was pretty in a way that made Zen think of mothers' magazines. She was wearing makeup, and had earrings on that matched her blouse. She also wore a gold cross pendant around her neck, hanging just above a demure top button. "Hello, Zenobia," she said warmly. "I'm very pleased to meet you."

"Thank you, ma'am. I'm pleased to meet you too," Zen managed. She was disconcerted by Mrs. Martin's eyes. They were bright, not unlike the Aunties', but also with a quirky thing at the corners that was like a secret smile. Her mouth had a quirky thing too. Zen had seen it before, at church back in Arizona. It said, I am a person who knows what I know.

"Would you like something to drink? We're a big soda family."

"Yes, please, ma'am."

In moments a fizzing glass was in her hand. There were bowls and plates of snacks around too.

"I really am pleased to meet you, you know," said Mrs. Martin, watching all the time with those quirky eyes. "When Melissa told me she had made a new friend, I thought, well, praise the Lord. It's been a little difficult to find like-minded people since we moved here."

Melissa said, "We came from Pennsylvania."

Zen cleared her throat. "I just moved here too," she said.

"Really?" said Mrs. Martin. "Where did you live before?"

"Arizona. A little town called Westfall."

"I don't know it."

Zen had no response to this.

"Well, no matter. And what does your father do?"

Zen dropped her eyes.

"Oh, dear, have I said something wrong?"

"Um . . . he was a contractor . . . but . . . um . . . he died."

"Oh, sweetheart, I'm so sorry! I didn't know. What about your mother, then?"

Zen wanted to twist away, but there was nowhere to go.

"Oh my Lord, you don't mean to say . . . you're an orphan?"

Zen's eyes stung. To hear it just said like that. Then to her startlement she was enfolded in cool, crinkly fabric and pressing arms. Mrs. Martin was hugging her. "Oh, sweet Jesus," the woman whispered. "You poor, poor dear."

So many feels, so fast, all at war with each other. Old grief suddenly sharp again. The anxiety to bend her lower body away from the body pressing hers, to keep Melissa's mother from feeling something she couldn't be allowed to feel. And, unexpectedly, a strong urge to hug back, to wrap her arms around this stranger woman and sob out all her pent-up pain. She made a choking sound.

Mrs. Martin hunkered down to bring their faces close. Melissa was watching, looking close to tears herself. What a warmhearted family this was. "Sweetheart, I'm so sorry," Mrs. Martin said. "I didn't mean to pry. But I'm glad you told me." A slight hesitation, and then, "So now you live with your . . . ?"

"My aunt Lucy."

"The woman who dropped you off."

"Yes, ma'am."

Mrs. Martin looked searchingly into Zen's face. "Well, then, I'm sure that's what the Lord intends. But, sweetheart, you should know, you always have a haven here if you need one."

"Thank you?" Zen said. She meant the gratitude, but was also squirming some. Things had gotten weirdly intense.

Mrs. Martin seemed to feel the same, because she stood up again and became brisk. "My goodness," she said. "Not exactly first-acquaintance talk. But no matter. You are welcome here. Are you ready for some word-game fun?"

"Yes, ma'am."

"Good. Because the little ones, they like the simpler games, but Melissa and I, we prefer to exercise our brains a bit more. Don't we, sweetheart?"

"Yes, Mother." They moved to the table where the board and racks and bag full of letter tiles had been set out.

Melissa and her mom kept up a lively flow of chitchat while they played, but they were both playing to win, and Zen soon realized she was out of her league. Half the words on the board she had never seen before. The first game came down to the last word, with Melissa thinking she was going to win until her mom's last big play, and, for the first time that Zen had seen, Melissa showed some temper: an angry word, a punch on a knee, and shiny eyes. This display earned Melissa a parental rebuke, which she sulked under. She shot her eyes at Zen, and Zen felt called upon as a friend in a way she wasn't sure she understood. She did her best to come up with a way to hold her face that expressed solidarity.

They played several games. Zen fidgeted and started glancing at the clock. It had been very kind of Melissa to invite her over, and her family was so pleasant. Still, as the hour of five approached, Zen found herself silently urging the minute hand around the clock face, and she felt a tightness in her chest loosen when, a few minutes before the top of the hour, she saw out the window that Aunt Lucy's car was pulling up to the curb.

TWENTY-ONE

Hello, God.

> *Today, game day at Melissa's house. It reminded me of home.*
>
> *Is it wrong, or sick, if I miss home?*
>
> *It was killing me. But I still miss it.*
>
> *Hey, God? If you care so much about me, why did you make me like this? Having to choose between being home and being real?*
>
> *This hurts so bad I wish I could just die.*
>
> *I miss Mom. I wish she had lived longer, so I could remember more.*
>
> *I do remember some.*
>
> *I remember that she was gentle.*
>
> *I remember she sang me to sleep at night.*
>
> *I remember her reading to me.*
>
> *I remember her putting medicine on my scraped knee, and a bandage.*
>
> *I remember her teaching me to pray.*
>
> *I remember food she made.*

Hot dogs and mac and cheese.

Meatloaf.

Grapefruit halves with sugar spooned on.

The cookies she baked. Gingersnaps. Crispy rice squares.

But I also remember the time I asked her if I could try her earrings and lipstick, and she said no, because you, God, you made me a boy, and those things were for girls.

And I didn't know how to say that that couldn't be right, because I wasn't a boy, at all.

Not then, not now, not ever.

Why couldn't I say?

Seriously, why?

Because I was FIVE!

I was afraid.

I wasn't strong enough.

I just didn't know how to put it into words.

And

And now

Now I never get to show her who I am—

Whispering these last words up at the dim ceiling of her bedroom, Zen could no longer keep her sobs quiet. Quick steps. A gentle knock. "Pumpkin?" said Aunt Phil's voice, muffled through the door. "You all right?"

Zen lay in bed and wailed. The door opened. Her craggy aunt came in, and Zen was startled to see through the prisms of her own tears that Aunt Phil's eyes were wet too. Aunt Phil wrapped her arms around her. "Oh, boo-boo," she murmured. "Oh, honeybunch. Chickadee. It's going to be all right."

Aunt Phil smelled different from Mrs. Martin. Less like perfume, more like a human with a human body. Neither of them smelled like Zen's mother, though. She couldn't remember anymore what her mother had smelled like, but she knew it was different from anyone else.

Not that it mattered. Her mother was long dead, and there was nothing she could do about it. Zen leaned into the comforting solidity of her murmuring aunt and howled out a small portion of her long-stored hurt.

TWENTY-TWO

THEY WERE TAKING a field trip to a radio station. A community station, it was called. Not like the Q or the Wolf or the River, but a place where volunteers did the shows. Mr. Walker had gotten them in because he did a show there himself. Radio was another geekery, it seemed. So many geekeries in the world. The station was near the school, at the university where Aunt Lucy worked.

Zen was one of the first on the bus, and took a seat half-way back. As soon as she was settled she saw Robert and a friend making their way down the aisle. She laid her hand across the seat next to her and looked pointedly out the window. She heard them go by and sit somewhere in back.

Eyes front again, and she saw Elijah just reaching the top of the steps. Gizmo? Nah. Elijah. He hadn't seemed to like the name, and Arli wasn't here. He gave Zen a look and a nod both so subtle that Zen felt sure no one else on the bus had seen them. He really was very good at making himself invisible. What was that word of Arli's? Chima. Elijah was an invisibility chima.

With a look, she invited him to sit beside her, and he did. That one act of extroversion accomplished, though, he immediately vanished again into a book.

Fine. Zen watched out the window, marveling again at all the green. It was almost indecent somehow. Vulgar. All those leaves. Trees showing off, shouting lookitme, lookitme!

A short drive, and the bus pulled up on a quiet street. Mr. Walker's class poured out onto the sidewalk next to an ordinary-looking white house.

At least, ordinary-looking on the outside. Inside was a space that reminded Zen of her dad's workshop: full of clutter, but with the feel that it was because work was getting done. There were stickers all over the place. Some of them were station bumper stickers—WYZA!—but there were also lots of bizarre arty stickers with random words on them. The names of bands, Mr. Walker said. Zen looked for a name she knew, but didn't see any. She recognized the music pumping from the speakers, though. Vintage country, just like she had been listening to the other night. She began to feel interested in this place.

The radio station man was a grizzled guy with a lot of mixy white-and-black hair bushing down toward his shoulders. He had a deep mellow voice and a way of rubbing his hands together, and Zen could tell from how he talked that he loved his station and his work.

First stop on the tour was a little room with a round table with microphones on it. Feeling crowded, Zen allowed others' jostling forward to shuffle her back, and ended up leaning against the wall next to, no surprise, Elijah. Of course back by the wall was where Elijah would be. Invisibility chima at work.

The man was talking about how bands played live in this room. "Hey," Zen whispered.

"Hi," Elijah whispered back.

Putting into words a growing feeling, Zen said, "This place is pretty cool, don't you think?"

Elijah nodded. He seemed like he might be solemn most of the time. "I have been here before," he said.

"Really?"

"Yes. There is a show on Tuesday evenings that is done by students our age. I have been on that show three times."

"That sounds amazing!"

"You can play—" Elijah began, and then pointed with his eyes toward the radio station man, who was saying, "You can play whatever songs you want and talk on the microphone and also say whatever you want, except no swears." Students laughed. "This is community radio, so everyone has a voice." He went on to explain that if you wanted to be on the show— *Tween You and Me*, it was called—all you had to do was show up at the right time on Tuesday evening. Zen made a mental note to tell the Aunties she wanted to come. Also, Arli would probably like it too.

The tour continued. There was a room lined with shelves

from floor to ceiling, and every shelf was crammed full of CDs. In the basement, on more shelves squeezed in under the exposed pipes, were vinyl records.

And then there was the Control Room, where the actual radio was made. The whole class stood breathless and still at the back of the room while the person who was on the air, a tall, straight-backed man with a baseball cap, did a "break." That meant he put on headphones and flipped a switch that made the music go mute and a big "On Air" light illuminate on the wall above his head, and then he leaned close to the microphone on its robot arm and talked. He announced the music and did the weather forecast and then pushed a button and turned off the microphone and a new song was playing.

The announcer turned his chair around and greeted the students. He had a courtly way of speaking. He talked about how on this station they got to play music nobody listened to anymore, and then, like he was proving his point, he said, "For example, I bet none of you has ever heard of the man singing right now. Anyone know who he is?" He seemed to think he already knew no one would, because he drew breath to speak again, but then he saw Zen's hand. "Yes, young lady?" he said.

Zen blushed happily at *young lady*. "Um, it sounds like Ernest Tubb to me," she said.

The man's face lit up. "Why, yes," he said. "That's exactly right." Eyes turned to look, and Zen's happy blush deepened. What her dad would have thought of the moment she couldn't even begin to guess.

Geeky lure, stronger now. This place was wicked cool.

The Control Room was the end of the tour. In the front room again, the radio station man did questions and answers and handed out bumper stickers. Then the class gathered on the front steps for a picture. Zen was feeling good: warm sun, maybe getting to be friends with Elijah, the Ernest Tubb moment, a new fun thing to think about doing. So it was like getting a bucket of cold water dumped over her when she heard snickering behind her and turned to see Robert and his friend both holding their shirt necks up around their ears. When he saw that she was looking, Robert made what she had to assume he thought was a funny expression, sucking his chin back, rolling his eyes, tottering his head back and forth.

Zen scowled. Her malice spiked, and the word was out before she could consider the consequences: "Mice."

Robert's face snapped back to its usual superior expression. They stared into each other's eyes. His widened. She closed her own and turned forward again. Had she given herself away? Had he seen that it had been her who had sabotaged his gameplay? Her face burned.

During the ride back to school she continued to squirm. Logical brain said, He couldn't possibly know it was me. He was talking about it in the cafeteria, so it makes total sense that I just overheard. But logical brain could not fully damp down the sick twist she felt in her stomach.

On the other hand, she had scored her point. There had been sweetness in the moment, no denying. And she had all the new clothes now. The insult no longer applied.

On her way back inside the school, she checked her reflection in the mirrored door. She was wearing the top with the huge flower today, plus the capris and cute sandals. She smiled a tight little smile of defiance. Let them mock. Even through the self-doubt Robert had triggered, she could see that she was looking good today.

TWENTY-THREE

Hello?

Helloooo

Yelloooooo

Felloooooooo

Melloooooo Jellooooooo
Smileeeee Face-eeeeeee!

Um, hello. What's up with you?

Just in a silly mood at the moment, is all.
Lafffeeeeee Face-eeeeee!

So I see. Should I be concerned?

Why?

You're right. I guess you just feel all the feels.

Yes, I do.

Riding the roller coaster, all the time.

OK then. So, what has you feeling so happy?

All kinds of things.
New clothes.
Ernest Tubb.
Uncle Sprink.

Who?

He's a friend of my aunts.
He took me shopping.
He's a drag queen.

I love it!

"Sprink" is short for Sprinkles La Fontaine.

EEEEE!

What is that?

Me squeeing. What a fantastic drag name.

He doesn't look much like a woman.

You'd be amazed what you can do
with makeup and clothes. And attitude.

You're an expert, I guess.

I suppose you could say that.
I take an interest.

Why?

Is it because you . . .

Because I what?

Well, I haven't wanted to ask.
I thought it might be rude.

But we're getting to be friends, right?

Yeah?

So, as a friend, can I just ask,
what gender are you?

You can ask.
And the answer is, kinda both kinda neither.

"Genderqueer"

That's right.
Good for you, knowing that word.

I've seen it online.

So can I ask you another question?

Maybe?

Because I've heard other people
talking about you once or twice,
and I heard them use certain words.

Stop!

What?

Don't type any of the words you mean.

Why not?

If you have to ask that, then you don't get it.

Don't get what?

What "genderqueer" means.

OK, fine. How about if you explain it to me?

It means, I feel in between,
in a way that's specifically different
from either endpoint.

And, yeah, of course I was born one way,
as far as my body goes, so I've always been
thought of that way by the people around me.

Still are, from the words I've heard.
The ones you stopped me from typing.

Well, yes. Because I haven't started
trying to get people to change yet.

So for now I'm just letting teachers
and other kids at school say the old words,
even though I hate it.

OK, so, next question.

Could we stop talking about this now please?

Why?

Because it's a hard thing for me to talk about.

OK?

OK, sure, no problem.

Thank you.
Now, I have a question.

Yes?

When do I get to meet your aunts?

Oh, right!

I've been meaning to tell you.
They said I could invite you over.

Huge grin face! *jumps up and down*

Would this Friday be OK?

Hold on, I'll ask.

Dum de dum de dum

How many angels can dance
on the head of a pin?

That's a thing my mother used to say . . .

I don't know why I remembered.

I can come!

Took you long enough.

Well, yeah. It's tricky sometimes.

What's tricky?

Talking to my dad. But we're cool.

OK, good.

TWENTY-FOUR

WEDNESDAY IN THE food court, Zen felt like a ball in a pinball machine. Every time she turned around someone else was there. Bounce! First it was Natalie, alone for once, seeming almost regular human-sized without her posse to back her up. Zen turned away from the burger station and found herself face to face with the haughty alpha girl. In the first moment, as they locked eyes, Zen resisted the urge to look down to remind herself what she was wearing. She made herself remember instead. What had she picked? Jeans and the pretty feminine top with the lace around the neck and the cute sandals. Yes! The outfit looked good, and she knew it. Natalie's eyes flicked down and up again, and her eyebrows lowered menacingly, but she did not speak. Zen twitched one eyebrow in response—What, nothing to say?—and brushed past, rejoicing inside.

Before she could properly savor the win, though, bounce! Melissa was there. Zen stutter-stepped to a halt. All week, every time they met, Melissa had been talking to her in a way that was clearly based on an idea that they were best friends now, and that, as such, of course they would always talk when they met, and of course it would go on as long as it could. Zen had taken to organizing her things in the last five minutes at the end of Mr. Walker's class and bustling out the door as soon as the bell rang, putting on a show of hurry, to avoid getting snared again.

"Hi!" Melissa said.

"Hi."

"Hey, I've been meaning to tell you, we decided we're not doing game day this weekend, because we're going on a family field trip, but you can come on that if you want. You want to come?"

"Um . . ."

Melissa's expectant smile vanished, but before either of them could speak again, bounce! Arli materialized at Zen's elbow, so suddenly it made her jump. She watched her two friends give each other hostile looks. Then Melissa spun away with a disdainful swish of her long blond hair.

"Game day?" said Arli, sounding snide.

"Um, yeah . . . I went over to her house last weekend. Her family does a thing with—"

"Why do you even talk to her?" Arli interrupted. "She's weird."

"You know, that's funny. She said the same thing about you."

But, before Arli could respond, bounce! Over Arli's shoulder, Zen saw an unexpected but so welcome face appear: Dyna. Zen uttered a shriek of joy, and Arli turned to look. Then the friend-triangle tension was forgotten in the hubbub of a happy reunion. All talking at once, they made their way to the usual table, where Clem was just sitting down, and the original quartet of the first day's orphan misfits was once again complete. As the greeting-chatter wound down, Zen said, "So, your dad let you come back?"

Dyna gave Zen a steady look before answering, and Zen smiled, seeing in the other girl's face what she felt herself, that since the mall encounter they were more connected. "Not exactly," said Dyna. Zen raised her eyebrows. "I told him that I was coming. I explained that to act from fear, it is to let fear vanquish you."

"*Vanquish*," said Arli reverently. "What a great word."

Clem said, "That takes some guts, telling your parents how it's going to be like that."

Dyna lifted her chin. "I am Chantal Kasongo," she said.

Clem said, "Well, I'm sold. When you run for president, I'll vote for you."

That got a laugh from Zen and Arli, but Dyna did not laugh. "I do not dream of being president," she said. Clem opened his mouth, but before he could speak, Dyna went on, "I am going to be a senator."

Arli and Clem both laughed again, clearly assuming this was also a joke, and Zen smiled, but she didn't laugh. She and

Dyna exchanged another look, and Zen nodded, acknowledging the determination she saw in the other girl's dark, fabric-framed face. A girl who told her parents what was what. A girl who calmly stated that she was going to be a senator someday. Not wanted to be. Was going to be. It was thrilling to see.

Humbling, too. Zen's eyes faltered and she looked away, then busied herself with her lunch. She frowned inside at her sudden dimming of mood. Only minutes ago she had been savoring a victory over queen bee Natalie. Now she was berating herself for not measuring up to her friend. As the joking and laughing of the table found its natural rhythm again, Zen whispered too quietly for her friends to hear, "I did the best I could. How was I supposed to tell them? I couldn't even say it to myself, hardly." And then, surprising herself both with the Lord's name in vain and the thought, "God damn it, I feel broken."

But that was too awful an idea to face for more than an instant. Zen turned back toward the warm connection happening among the other three humans at the table.

TWENTY-FIVE

AS THE DINNER with Arli approached, Zen began to feel uneasy. The evening before, listening to a blues show streaming from WYZA and doing her homework in her room, she realized why. She needed to talk to the Aunties.

She took her headphones off and listened to the voices on the other side of the door. Just the two of them tonight, for a change—no company. She was becoming more familiar with the tones and variations of both of their voices. Aunt Lucy, when she got going, sounded like someone giving a lecture. She could talk as long as no one else interrupted. When Aunt Phil talked, it was shorter, but also more . . . jazzy, or something. Funky rhythms. Zen liked both of their voices. They matched her deepening sense of who they were as people.

And, time to do this. Zen took a deep breath, put her shoulders back, tugged the ends of her hair down toward her shoulders (almost touching on their own now), and opened the door.

Aunt Lucy was speaking, but found a place to stop. "Something up, Zenobia?" she said. "Are we talking too loudly?"

Yes, but not what Zen had come to say. "No, it's okay," she said. Then her tongue went leaden, and she faltered into silence.

"Everything all right, boo-boo?" asked Aunt Phil. Both Aunties looking concerned now.

"Yes, m— Yes, thank you." More silence. "Um." Yet more silence. She took a shaky breath and said, "Arli doesn't know."

"Doesn't know what?" said Aunt Lucy.

"About . . . you know. About how I lived before."

"Ah," said Aunt Lucy. Aunt Phil was nodding.

"Actually, I don't think anyone at school knows yet," said Zen.

"That was how you wanted it," said Aunt Lucy.

Indeed. Through the spring and summer there had been a series of discussions, out of which had come decisions. The decision to live full-time. The decision to pursue treatment. And the decision to tell absolutely no one about Zen's past life. *Living in stealth*, it was called.

"Yes," Zen said. "That was how I wanted it." She groped for words. "It's just . . . I didn't realize how hard it would be. Doing girl every day. I mean, I really am one, but still, I don't have any practice. And I'm so afraid they're going to find out."

Aunt Phil held out her arms, and Zen went to her. The hug felt so good it made her eyes leak some. She wiped at them and went on. "So tomorrow night, when Arli is here . . . I mean, I like Arli a lot, and I wouldn't mind them knowing, but it just seems safer to keep it secret from everyone for a while longer. If we can." A breathing pause. "Okay?"

"Sure, Zenobia," said Aunt Lucy. "Not to worry. We'll keep you safe."

"Thank you." Enough hugs for now, comforting though they were. Zen stepped out of Aunt Phil's arms.

"You said 'them,'" said Aunt Lucy.

"Yes, I caught that too as it flittered by," said Aunt Phil.

"I'm sorry?"

"For your friend. You used the pronoun 'them,'" said Aunt Lucy.

"Oh yes, that's right. Arli is, I think the word is 'gender-queer'?"

"Ah," said Aunt Lucy, at the same time that Aunt Phil said, "Far out."

Aunt Lucy said, "I very much look forward to meeting this young person."

Aunt Phil was smiling her twisty smile. "Me too," she said. "Right on. Groovy. Let's assemble."

On her way back into her room, Zen paused and turned back. "And, um, one more thing?"

Aunt Lucy said, "Yes?"

"Um, would it be all right . . . What I mean is, for this dinner . . . could we have normal food for once?" She blushed, but didn't drop her eyes.

The Aunties glanced at each other. Aunt Phil snorted and said, "All right, chickadee, I'll see what I can come up with."

TWENTY-SIX

THE EVENING OF, as arrival-time approached, Zen asked
Aunt Lucy for permission to go wait out front on the curb.
"Of course, Zenobia," Aunt Lucy said, looking startled to be
asked.

The apartment house was on a quiet street. No cars for
minutes at a time. The top of the hour came and went. Zen
fidgeted. Just as she began to think that maybe Arli wasn't
going to show, a faded silver minivan rounded the corner. A
thumping bass-beat accompanied it. Arli was clearly visible in
the passenger seat. The driver was a boy who looked to be
of high school age. He had the beginnings of facial hair, a
fair amount of acne, and a scowl. Zen stepped to the curb.
The minivan pulled up, throbbing. The door opened and Arli
climbed out.

Once standing, Arli turned back and said to the driver,
"Thanks." Not sounding particularly thankful.

The driver didn't look particularly thanked. "You got a ride home, right?" he said.

"Yeah."

Without saying another word, driver boy immediately started rolling the vehicle forward, forcing Arli to scramble to close the door. The moment it was shut the van revved and leapt away. A moaning of tires, and it was out of sight around the far corner.

"Hi," said Zen, feeling distressed. Unwilling witness to family friction.

"Hey," Arli said, still staring darkly after the departed minivan.

"Was that your . . ." said Zen.

"My brother," Arli said. A beat. "His name is Lester." Another beat. "Which is short for, 'The Less Said About Him the Better.'" They started up the steps. Arli said, "Do you think your rentsibs would adopt me?"

The heartfelt tone of the question knocked Zen off-kilter. "Maybe, I guess?" she said. A clunky reach for banter: "We'd have to share a room."

"Fine with me," said Arli.

Inside, the Aunties said warmly welcoming things, and Arli answered them in a way that sounded hungry, somehow. A yearning toward. To break the smiling but awkward silence after intros, Zen said, "How is 'Lester' short for 'The Less Said About Him the Better'?"

Arli said, "First few letters plus last few letters. The L-E-S from 'Less' and the T-E-R from 'Better.'"

"It's the exact opposite of how you did your nickname."

"Yes! Thank you for noticing!"

They moved into the kitchen. Pasta sauce bubbled on the stove, steaming pungent garlic and oregano. A big green salad sat next to a bowl of bread. They took their seats, and Aunt Phil brought heaping plates of spaghetti.

As they began to eat, Aunt Lucy said to Arli, "That's interesting, how you made 'Lester' out of that phrase. A fruitful game with my name, too, I think."

Arli was instantly intent. "What is your name?"

"Lucille Abigail Jarecky."

"AAAAAHH!" said Arli. "That is just so Fan. Tas. Tic! Lucky! Rentsib Lucky!"

Aunt Lucy smiled, and said, "'Rentsib'? That's a curious word."

"It's short for 'parent sibling.' It's a word my parent uses."

Zen said, "You told me before you made it up."

Arli's response was a pained look: How could you be so crass as to call me on that? No chance to talk about it, though, because Aunt Phil said, "Your parent? Not 'Mom' or 'Dad'? 'Cause I'm noticing, young human, you don't use a lot of gendered words at all."

Arli gaped at Aunt Phil, then turned to Zen and said, "I love your rentsibs. Just absolutely love them." Then, back to the Aunties: "That's exactly right. It's another thing my parent taught me. Vo has this idea of taking gender out of language completely."

Aunt Lucy said, "'Vo'?"

"My parent's own gender-neutral pronouns. Vo-ven-veir. Instead of he-him-his, or she-her-hers. I made them—I mean, I wish I had made them up. But they come from my dad's family, from his heritage. Which is weird, because it's my other parent who's into it. Anyway, it's a thing that goes back generations."

"Fascinating," said Aunt Lucy. "What heritage is that?"

"Nezelia, is the name of the country. It doesn't exist anymore."

Aunt Lucy looked skeptical, but didn't say anything.

Zen, feeling left out, said, "What about my name? How would you first-bit last-bit that?"

Arli's eyes went off into the corner while vo calculated. "No super-cool combos, I'm afraid," vo said. "I guess 'Zenly' is the best you can do."

Aunt Phil said, "Meaning, in a Zen fashion. 'I meditate, but I don't meditate zenly.'"

Aunt Lucy laughed. "'They were annoying me, but I tried to respond to them zenly.'"

Arli mouthed silently to Zen, *love love love.*

TWENTY-SEVEN

DURING DESSERT, WHICH was a vegan lemon cake Aunt Lucy had baked—once in a while, Zen had to admit, their weird food was yummy—Aunt Phil pointed her shrewd, kind eyes at Arli and said, "So, an older brother about whom the less said the better, and an ungendered parent who wasn't raised that way, and a dad who was. Sounds like there's a lot of story there."

Arli's face clouded. Vo leaned back in veir chair. "Um, well, yes."

"No pressure, dumpling, but, feel like telling some of it?" A silence. "Because, what you got yourself here is some sympathetic ears."

Arli did a slow look around the table. "Well, I don't mind talking about it, I guess," vo said. Another thought-gathering pause. Then, "Okay, so, my parents got divorced a couple years ago—honestly, I can't understand why they ever got married—and now my parent lives in a trailer park in Scarborough, and my dad lives here in town. And my brother and I live with my dad most of the time, because our schools are here, and because he has an actual house." Arli's eyes dropped. Veir fingers fiddled with the edge of the table. "My brother and my parent don't talk to each other anymore, so there's no more going back and forth for him, but I still go and stay with ven in veir trailer some weekends and holidays and for a while during the summer." More fiddly silence. Some kind of tough feels happening. Zen reached out and touched Arli's shoulder. "I don't like my dad much. Or my brother at all. But my mom . . . dang it, my parent, isn't exactly a stable-home sort of person either, so . . . so, it's not so good sometimes, these days."

Zen did another shoulder-touch, and Aunt Phil said, "Sweetums. It can be tough, for sure."

"They don't . . . my father and brother, they don't believe in the Nezel gender stuff, about how you can be in between, and vo-ven-veir and all that. They think it's stupid. But it has always made complete and total sense to me, and I just know. This is me. I just know."

Zen bit her lip and had to look away. Such strong parallels to her own experience. She ached to say so. But.

Arli did an eye-rolly laugh. "So anyway," vo said, "that's more than I was planning to tell you about the soap opera that is my life." Vo turned abruptly to Zen. "How about you? What was your family like? Your old family, in Arizona?"

Aunt Lucy gave Zen a look that said plainly, You don't have to if you don't want to.

But she did want to. As much as she could, anyway. She cleared her throat. "Okay, so I told you my parents are dead." Arli nodded, solemn. "My mom died when I was five. She got cancer. And my dad, I told you, had a hunting accident. They said." A look went around the table. Or suicide, no one said, but Zen had thought it before, and she could see in Aunt Lucy's face that she had too. "We lived in a little town called Westfall. My dad was a contractor and my mom did a bunch of different home business stuff while she took care of me. And we were, I guess you could say, a pretty religious family. Church every Sunday, and most Wednesday nights, too, and Bible study on Saturdays." It was getting harder to say more without getting into hints about gender. "And . . . my parents stayed married. Until my mom died. It was after that that my dad really got a little . . . that he went deeper into the religious stuff, and started to . . . started"—groping for a finish—"well, um . . . I guess I'd just say that you can believe me when I say that I also know what it's like to live with a parent who sees things differently from you."

Feeling so ready to be done talking, Zen got up to put her cake plate by the sink. That got lighter after-dinner talk going, and the rest of the visit and the giving of a ride home passed without further unplanned dives into deeper emotional waters.

Hello, God.

I wanted to tell Arli more tonight, so bad. But I was too afraid. My old life—it's all mixed up together, and I feel like, if I tell one thing, everything will come out. And I like Arli a whole lot, but I'm just not ready to tell anyone about being the way I am.

Even with the awkward parts, though, tonight was really nice. Every once in a while, when I can stop bracing for disaster, I feel like maybe things are actually going to be okay here.

But I also keep coming back to that old life. How it wasn't all bad. The last time I talked to you, I was remembering good stuff about Mom. Talking to Arli made me remember good things about Dad, too.

Like, in his workshop, first big-kid project, and it was this special deal, making a stool. I did each step so carefully: cutting the top board and the leg pieces, making sure the grain was up and down on the leg pieces, instead of sideways, because if it was sideways, it might snap when someone sat on it. Then getting to actually use the band saw, and cutting out the place where the leg pieces went in with a chisel and that big weird chisel hammer thing, and then the wedge-pegs and glue, and getting to use the thingy to make the design in the edge around the top, what was it called? A router. That's funny. That word means something completely different now. Gotta tell Arli. Anyway, using the router to make the edge design, and then sanding and staining, and it really came out good, and Dad was proud. He did that fakey voice from an old movie or something—oh no—and he said, "Dat's my boy!"

Damn it, why can't I just enjoy a memory for once? I hate this, God. I can't go back to my old life without the boy-girl thing jumping up like a shark into a boat and wrecking everything.

But, I made my choice, so I guess I just have to live with it.

And that seems like a bad note to end on, but I don't have anything else to say to you right this moment. I mean, bless everybody and all that, always, but beyond that, you know what? I'm done for now.

TWENTY-EIGHT

ENTERING MR. WALKER'S classroom Monday morning of the fourth week of school, feeling good—the roller coaster up today—Zen saw Melissa's inviting-face and, following the impulse of the moment, took the desk next to hers. Melissa watched her approach eagerly, and, as soon as Zen sat down, put something on her desk. It was made of thread, thin and floppy, with a woven-together part down the middle, knots outside that, and loose strings past the knots on both ends. It was yellow and blue and green. It was pretty.

Zen gave Melissa a questioning look, and Melissa actually blushed. Zen had never seen her do that before. "It's a friend-ship bracelet," Melissa said. "I made it for you."

Zen looked back down, and a sudden warmth rushed through her. A present made by hand, and offered with a blush. How sweet. But, even with almost no experience with girl stuff like this, Zen knew her window to have this go well was tiny. No hesitation. Respond, now. "Oh, wow. Cool!

Thank you," she said. "You made this? Yourself?" A nod. Zen didn't have to fake the smile. She felt it blossoming on her face. The little head-duck and eyelid-flutter came intuitively too. "That's so nice of you! Thank you!"

"You really like it?"

"Yes. I love it. Thank you!"

Melissa blushed again. Thanks delivered. It had been real. And the glow Zen felt, the smile as she held out her wrist for Melissa to tie the bracelet on, they were real too. The call and response of girl-friending could be complicated, but it did seem to come naturally.

When the bell rang at the end of class, Mr. Walker caught her eye, so she went over to his desk. "Zen," he said. "I finally had a chance to talk to the rest of the website committee, and I think I've convinced them that a tracker, like you suggested, is worth a try."

Zen nodded. Good.

"The thing is," Mr. Walker went on, "we have no idea what program to use, and we were hoping . . . but I see you already have an idea about that."

"Yes," said Zen. She had given the matter some thought. Her first choice would have been to use a really tight and clever piece of coding by one of her old acquaintances on the dark web, but there was no point mentioning that. Instead she had looked into the consumer-grade options out there and found one that seemed solid. A smaller company. Little one-person startup, looked like. "I think I might know what you need," she said, and, taking a pen and sticky notepad from his desk, she wrote down a URL. "Easy to install and check." Another bell rang. Zen responded quickly to her teacher's thanks and hurried to her next class.

At lunch Arli gave the friendship bracelet a hard stare, but didn't say anything. Thank God for small favors. No one else was at the table yet. After they had both said hi, an awkward silence fell. Texting hadn't happened over the weekend, so it was the first time they had communicated since the unexpectedly deep feels of the dinner on Friday. Zen was engaged in a minute examination of her fork when Arli said, "Um, I really liked your rentsibs." Zen looked up. "A lot."

Zen nodded, looked down again. "They liked you too," she said. "Obviously."

Arli hesitated. Then, "That thing I said about adopting . . . I could tell you didn't like that."

"No, it's okay."

"I was joking, of course. I mean, you know that, right?"

"Yeah, I know."

They were looking at each other again now, both still a little flinchy-shy, but the feels were getting better. "I just . . . I sure would like to talk to them some more sometime."

"Okay."

"I mean, not right away, or whatever. I'm not fishing. I just felt . . . at home. For the first time." A pondering pause. "Ever."

A little irked, Zen said, "They're not perfect, you know."

Arli gave her a doubting look.

Zen looked away. The image had risen in her mind of Mrs. Martin, and of the solid, for lack of a better word, *normalness* of the Martins' house. A house with a woman and a man in it being a mom and a dad. A house where everyone was so sure about what was right and what was wrong, and that they were right. There was a feeling of sweet, simple certainty in that. She knew it from her old life, and it had its lure.

Even if one of the things they might think they knew was wrong was Zen, if they knew.

Or Arli, for that matter, with veir in-betweeny thing.

Or maybe Clem, with his half-and-half blue hair and tie-dyed shirt. Clem, who was coming across the cafeteria toward them and sitting down. He looked troubled.

Arli said, "We were just talking about parents. Or guardians."

"Yeah?" said Clem.

"What's it like at your house? How do the 'rents feel about your blue hair?"

"My mom let me do it originally, and pretends to be cheerful about it, but keeps dropping little hints. And my dad couldn't care less. About anything, much." These remarks delivered in a flat voice. Zen was momentarily distracted by faces pointed toward her from over at the popular kids' table. Natalie was looking right at her, and when their eyes met, Natalie put her index fingers up over her eyebrows and wiggled them like inchworms crawling. The whole table burst out laughing. What?

"So, anyway," Arli began, but Clem interrupted. "Have you heard?"

"Heard what?" said Arli.

"It's all over the school," said Clem. "Remember that kid Elijah? Who sat with us last week?"

"Yeah, what about him?" Arli said.

Zen's eyes, returning to her friends, swept the gamer table and took in the fact that Robert was looking back and forth between herself and Natalie and laughing too.

"Well, turns out he's a girl. I mean, he was born with a girl body. He's transgender."

Zen gasped like she had been punched in the stomach.

"And when his family heard that the word was out, they kept him, I mean her, I mean him, home from school."

"Him," said Arli.

Zen clattered to her feet. Eyes, eyes, eyes! She could feel them everywhere. Stifling the shriek that wanted to burst from her body, she fled toward the bathrooms.

TWENTY-NINE

"WHAT'S TROUBLING YOU, Zenobia?"

"My stomach hurts. A lot." Nurse's office, and not lying, exactly. Her stomach did hurt. Just not because she was sick. There was no question in her mind, though: school was done for today. Inchworm fingers—whatever that meant, but obviously not anything good—and a trans kid getting outed, and now she needed to go home. But she couldn't say that to this nice lady. So, a little playacting was required. Zen clutched her abdomen and groaned. Not too much, though. Don't overplay it. Fortunately, the run to the bathroom and then on to here had left her red-faced, hot, and out of breath.

The nurse—Mrs. Lopez, her name was—put the back of her hand against Zen's forehead and said, "Do you have your monthlies yet?"

Zen looked blankly at her.

"Your period, hon. Do you have it yet? Could be cramps."

Zen continued to stare, then blushed deeply and stammered, "N-no, not yet."

Mrs. Lopez was not paying close attention. She clicked a mouse, then did some typing on her computer. She said, "Lucille Jarecky. Is that your mom?"

"No, ma'am," Zen said, still reeling from the period question. "My mom is . . . I mean, my parents . . . my parents are gone. Aunt Lucy is my guardian."

"Oh, I'm sorry," said Mrs. Lopez. But then right back to business. "Well, she's listed as your contact, so just lie still and breathe, hon, while I make a call. Do you want a glass of water?"

"Yes, please." Freak-outs were hot sweaty work.

Zen lay on the vinyl-covered couch-bed thing and watched the nurse stare at the wall as she listened to Aunt Lucy's cell ring. The phone squicked and her face came to life. "Yes, hello! Is this Mrs. Lucille Jarecky? It's Anita Lopez, the nurse at Monarch Middle School. I'm calling about Zenobia"—a glance at the computer screen—"July. You are her guardian, correct? Yes? Okay, that's fine. I'm calling because I have her here in my office, and she says she's not feeling well." Mrs. Lopez glanced again at Zen. Underplay, underplay. Zen let her eyes go unfocused and grimaced slightly. "Yes, stomach pain. Could be this bug that's been making the rounds here. Twenty-four-hour thing." Then the nurse was mostly nodding and um-humming, and Zen let her head fall back with a sigh. She was going to get to go home.

Mrs. Lopez hung up the phone and stated in a carefully neutral voice, "She said her wife is coming to get you." Her face had gone blank. Did she disapprove of women married to women? Anyway, she seemed to need convincing, so Zen said, "Yes, they're married. Aunt Lucy and Aunt, uh, Philomena."

Mrs. Lopez nodded one short nod, her face still flat and chilly. "Yes, that was the name," she said. Then she instructed Zen to lie still and went off into her computer again.

When Aunt Phil showed up, she did a thing Zen had never seen her do before, a kind of scrunched-up little smile and a careful way of talking, as though Mrs. Lopez was either a child, or someone who could cause a lot of trouble, or both. A gentle, laughy uber-politeness with lots of nodding. There was an awkward back-and-forth, but finally the nurse seemed to believe that all was on the level. Then Zen and Aunt Phil were walking home. The afternoon was cloudy and cool. It felt like autumn saying, Hold on a second there, summer, it's my turn.

They walked for a while without speaking, and then Aunt Phil said, "So, stomachache, huh?"

Zen glanced up. Her aunt's eyes seemed sunk deep in her face. "Yeah."

They walked a little farther. "What do you suppose caused it, tweetie-bird? Some kinda bug?"

Zen glanced again. Expression still unreadable. Suddenly she mistrusted that seamed face, those pointy-awl eyes. What do you care? she thought savagely. "The nurse said there's something going around." Silence. "Could we walk a little slower? I don't feel so good."

"Sure, honeybunch."

Zen took refuge in temper. "Why couldn't you have picked me up in the car?"

"Lu has it, scrumptious. And anyway, as I've mentioned, me and driving . . . not so much."

They walked the rest of the way back to the apartment without further speech. Once there, Zen went straight into her room and closed the door, brushing aside as she went Aunt Phil's bumbling words about food and water and medicine. She lay down on the bed and had a silent cry. Then she fell asleep.

When Aunt Lucy came home there was a different flavor of an adult not knowing what to do or say, and from the deeper layers of a mood quickly darkening, Zen observed them contemptuously. These people had no idea how to be parents. They had never done it. They didn't know anything about it. How could she have started to trust them? Effortlessly she deflected their feeble attempts to say helpful things, to find anything out, though she did accept the offer of soup and crackers on a tray. Once she had it, she closed the door in the Aunties' worried, solicitous faces. She slurped her soup, then turned to the machine. Cyberlandium beckoned.

Turn to the side first, though. As soon as she signed on, Arli was there.

THIRTY

Hey, Zen. Are you OK?

Hello? Are you there?
I see your green dot.

Yes I'm here

Uh-oh, no punctuation.
Now I'm really worried.

Hello?

What do you want
?

Do I have to want something to talk to you?

No, I guess not.

Whatever.

Somebody's in a mood.

So what if I am?

OK, fine. So you're in a mood.
What happened today?

You wouldn't understand.

Try me.

Hello?

Look, no offense,
but I haven't known you very long.

So?

So

So maybe I don't feel like
sharing every little thing.

OK, I'm going to take the chance and ask.
Was it the thing about that kid Elijah?

No

Because, if it was, I would suggest that you need to calm down. It's not a big deal.

I mean, you were cool about genderqueer that other time, but maybe you still need someone to tell you: Trans is real, and normal, and nothing to get worked up about.

That's not it at all.

No, listen, I think you really need to hear this.

Stop

I don't know what things were like back in Arizona, but if you want to learn how to be a good ally, which clearly you do, can I just suggest that maybe you need to do a little work here?

You are getting this so wrong right now

You don't have to get all defensive.

I'm not

Are you sure about that?

Hello?

Well, it doesn't matter.
I'm going to send you a couple of links.
Some 101 websites.

I can't even

And just, you know, a friendly suggestion
that you maybe try to put aside what you
learned back home and approach this with
an open mind?

Can I suggest that, as a friend?
OK?

Hello?

Hello?

THIRTY-ONE

DRIVEN BY THE black boil of feels inside her, Zen slammed into the Lukematon control room. The clang of the door hitting the wall ricocheted back down the grungy tunnel behind. Nobody there. Nobody ever there. And nobody understood her, nobody really knew her, nobody could be trusted. It was infuriating. She needed to wreak havoc on something, on someone. The old dark drive was back. Time to do some hurting.

It only took a second to confirm that Chopper789 was active in a game. Robert would do for a start. Him and his mean laughing face. And no kooky mouse-breathing dragon this time. She was going to erase him. No, she would torture him first. Turn his precious Vorpal Sword into a trout. Have NPCs insult him. Empty his satchel and fill it with rocks. Then she would totally erase him. She would expunge him from the platform, block him from ever playing again. But turning the sword into a fish, that was first.

Except, he wasn't in the D&D world where she had found him before. He was . . . Wait, really? That silly lollipop game? What was he doing in there?

Invisibly, she inserted herself into his playing environment. He was at one of the early puzzles, the wall with the maze on it, sliding the different colors of gumdrops around. And he was playing as a girl. His avatar had a dress and cute black shoes and anime hair.

What?

No.

Could Robert be trans too?

Zen pulled back from the laptop with a gasp. She sat, breathing heavily, and stared at this question in her mind. Then she shook her head. No, it was extremely unlikely that Robert was trans. Everything she had ever seen him do and say, all his ways of being, were just so obviously boy boy boy. Not his body. That didn't matter. How he did. He was a natural boy.

And yet he was playing a girl character in a game.

Which was totally common, she recalled, now that she was breathing and thinking again. She pictured a hulking muscle-bound warrior bristling with armor and weapons, pushing gumdrops around in the maze wall with the point of his spear, and snorted. And she had done it herself, of course. She ran a quick partial list in her mind of the many different aliases and avatars she had inhabited. There were plenty of both female and male. And some animals and a genderless plant creature and who knows what else.

So, okay, Robert was just playing. Fine. She could still wreak havoc on him. She could wreak havoc on anyone. It was her superpower. Except . . . hovering hand . . . except, she didn't want to, anymore. The tornado was spinning down. The mood-blackness still lurked, but it was shading over to sad now. The rage felt so good when she was down inside it, but it was hard to keep it going. Zen wondered if that meant she was weak somehow.

As a matter of form, just because it was so easy to do, she slid a couple of Robert's gumdrops back after he slid them forward. She switched two of them. Changed the color of one. Made one disappear. She sighed. With a click she increased the number of gumdrops tenfold, so that they jammed every channel of the maze and couldn't be budged. Then she sighed again and, with another click, returned his game to normal.

She sat for a bit, playing with her fingers. Kept wanting to paint her nails, kept forgetting. Another thing the Aunties were clueless about. Or at least, insufficiently enthusiastic. But was that their job? To cheerlead endlessly? Zen frowned, wondering if she had been too harsh before. Sure, they had no parenting experience. But they had taken her in and were trying to make her a home. Her throat tightened. It was just that they weren't . . . They could never replace . . . A tear tracked down her cheek.

A tap on the door. "Twiglet?" said Aunt Phil's voice. "You still in there?"

Zen made a wordless sound. Not angry. Just minimum effort to answer yes.

"May I come in?"

She wiped the tear away. "Mmm."

The door cracked open, and Aunt Phil stuck her face in. "I just wanted you to know, your aunt Lucy and I are going out. We have a meeting."

"Okay."

"How are you feeling now?"

"A little better, thanks."

"You sound tired, cupcake."

Zen looked at her aunt. "I *am* tired," she said. "So tired." She stared at her computer again, safely switched to an innocuous homework screen. "Tired like, a week's vacation can't even begin to touch this tired." She took in and blew out a shuddery breath.

"Well, we'll be back late, so why don't you start with at least one good night's sleep?"

"Yeah, okay."

"And you know, there's still some lemon cake in the fridge."

"Really? Okay. Thanks, Aunt Phil."

Aunt Lucy looked in over her wife's shoulder. "Feeling better?"

"A little, thanks. Aunt Phil told me about the lemon cake. I think I'm going to finish my homework, and have dessert, and maybe watch some of my show, and then sleep."

"Very good. I've got my phone if you need to reach me. We'll only be a short walk away." Then the SFX of gathering stuff, and out the door they went.

Ten minutes later Zen was in her nightgown, a plate with a large cube of cake on it balanced on her knees, and she had dimmed the lights to make the subtitles easier to read and had pulled up the latest episode—yo, ho, fiddledee-dee, everyone a pirate nowadays—on her favorite clearinghouse site. Time to disappear again for a little while into the marvelously convoluted plots and cyberpunky glamour of Kimazui.

So, yeah, God.

This kid Elijah at school: turns out he's trans. Too. And he got outed today, and I just couldn't handle it. I pretended to be sick and made them send me home.

And if I go back tomorrow, with everybody thinking about stuff like this, I mean, how can they not see? How can they not know? It just keeps happening that nobody sees and so I've kept going, but I'm always waiting for the hammer to fall, and I hate having this hammer hanging over my head. I HATE IT!

But if I don't go back, if I play sick again tomorrow, and again the day after that, first of all they're not going to believe me. And then, if I'm so afraid to go to school, to go anywhere, because somebody might figure out that I was born with a boy body, that I have this stupid thing between my legs that I hate with all my brain, then . . . then they win.

I'm so tired. And I'm so afraid. But I guess I have to try again. God damn it all to hell. And I don't care if that's taking your name in vain. God, Jesus, Lord, they're all just words. Mom would hate me saying that. Dad would scream at me. But that's how I feel right now, so that's what I said. Bless everyone, blah blah blah. That's all.

THIRTY-TWO

ZEN SPENT BREAKFAST on the edge of playing sick for another day, but when Aunt Lucy said, "It's time to go," she sighed and picked up her backpack. Okay, fine. What she would say when she saw Arli, she had no idea. She hoped it wouldn't be until lunch. If then.

But there were other challenges first, starting with Mr. Walker's class first period. It felt like even though the hallway was flat, it was getting steeper uphill with each step toward the classroom door. Who was already there? Which eyes would meet hers first? Her hand squeezed her backpack strap tight. She clenched her jaw and continued forward.

First eyes, one quick flick and away: Elijah. So, he had come to school today. That was brave. Zen's heart went out to him, all at once. She took a step toward him, wanting so much to offer comfort, support . . . but what could she say without risking exposure herself? Having a secret turned out to have a big problem attached to it. It made it practically impossible to stand with someone else who had the same secret.

Melissa's voice spoke behind her. "Sad."

Zen turned and faced her . . . friend? Were they friends, really? There had been some truly sweet moments. But, also, this feeling of not quite matching up. Zen asked, hoping her guess was wrong, "What's sad?"

"That girl. Thinking she's a boy." Not wrong, then. "And I guess her parents actually encourage it. I mean, look at her. Look at the clothes she's wearing. She didn't buy those by herself."

Zen's heart was whacking in her ears. She managed to say, "Himself."

"What?"

"Himself. He's a boy."

"No, she's not," said Melissa. "My mother says, people like that, they're just confused."

Mr. Walker saved Zen from having to answer this by calling the class to order. She turned her back on Melissa and found a desk closer to Elijah, who had drawn into a protective ball. All shields up.

At the end of class Mr. Walker once again caught her eye, so Zen made her way over to his desk. To her intense annoyance, Robert moved in the same direction.

"Zen," said Mr. Walker, "I just wanted to tell you, the website committee checked out your tracker, and it looked good, so we downloaded it and installed it."

Zen opened her mouth to answer, but didn't get to speak.

"Tracker?" said Robert. "What tracker?"

By his breezy tone, Mr. Walker was unaware of the tension zinging between the two students in front of him. "Zenobia here turns out to be quite the expert," he said. "She's helping us set up a, well, not exactly a trap, but a safety device, so that if the hacker strikes again, we'll have a way maybe to find out who it is."

Robert's mouth twisted. "I could have helped you with that," he said. His face looked like a storm moving in. The locked gazes crackled and fizzed.

Mr. Walker, rummaging in a desk drawer, was still oblivious. "I'm sure you could have," he said in a soothing voice.

Robert's face got darker, and he said, directly to Zen now, "How come you know so much about computers? Huh?"

On any other turf, Zen would have backed down. Not here. "What, you think nobody but you has skills?"

"Where are you even from? You're a really weird kid, you know that?"

This finally got Mr. Walker's attention. "Robert," he said. "That's no way to talk to a fellow student."

"Fellow student," Robert echoed. Zen felt her face go white. *Fellow.* That was a gendered word, that was. At least, sometimes. But was he using it that way? Robert's hand went up to his brow. His finger did inchworm motions.

Zen's face went hot. "What is that supposed to mean?"

"If you don't know, I'm not going to tell you."

Mr. Walker said, "What is going on here?" Both of his students ignored him.

Robert said, "Who *are* you?"

"Who are *you*?"

"Whoa!" Mr. Walker said, actually sounding sharp for once. "Time out." They both looked at him. "I don't know what's going on here, but it needs to stop. You two need to get to your next classes, and I need to teach mine."

Robert gave Zen one last hard glare, turned on a heel, and left.

At lunch, standing on the table-decision spot, Zen saw that Arli's table of orphan misfits was already packed. Arli, Clem, Dyna, a kid Zen didn't know, and Elijah were all there. Even without Elijah sitting right there, she couldn't bear the thought of another gender-lecture from Arli, so she headed for Siberia, as it was called—the farthest corner, where a few tables usually sat empty all lunch. She ate facing the wall and spoke to no one. Shields up. Walls in place. When the bell rang she sat another minute, letting the room empty out behind her before turning around. When she did, though, Natalie was still at her table, with her friend Olive. As soon as their eyes met, Natalie did the finger-wiggling thing again.

By this point in a very trying day, Zen was in just the right frame of mind, edgy and fierce, to deal with this straight on. She got up and walked over. Natalie watched her approach with a calm, superior expression. Olive gaped. Zen stopped in front of them and said, "What."

Natalie shrugged.

"That thing you're doing with your fingers," Zen said. Her voice came out low and steady. Almost like friends talking. The odd intimacy of enemies. "What's it supposed to mean?"

"It means," said Natalie just as evenly, "that you have freakishly bushy eyebrows. They look like caterpillars."

Olive burst out laughing.

"Big, ugly, hairy caterpillars."

Zen flushed and scowled. Olive was still laughing. Natalie contented herself with a smile, equal parts fake sweetness and real malice. There was a shutter sound effect. Olive had snapped another picture. Zen whirled and stomped away.

The caterpillar incident made an already dark day even darker, and Zen only barely managed to keep herself from arranging some new way to bail. Somehow, though, she persevered. At least she hadn't had to come face to face with Arli. She still had no idea how to work past the awful text exchange.

But then there was the part at the end of the day when Zen had just started walking home and Arli came panting up behind. "Hey," vo called. Zen kept walking. "Hey," again. Fine. Let's get this over with. She stopped and turned.

"What happened last night?" Arli said. "We got cut off."

"I don't know."

"And I forgot to send you stuff. But I will."

Zen groped without success for anything to say. Arli was already moving on. "And sorry about the table being full at lunch. I mean, we could have squeezed you in, but I get the feeling you don't like having too many people close to you at one time."

Wait, what? She had just settled it in her mind that, despite early indications to the contrary, vo was utterly clueless. Startled into speech, she said, "Um, that's right, actually. Thanks for noticing."

"You're welcome. But that's not why I wanted to talk to you." An expectant pause. "Well? Aren't you going to ask?"

The old rhythm—if anything could be called old between two people who had only known each other for a month. Despite herself, Zen smiled a little. "You like to be asked, don't you?"

"Why, yes, actually. Thank you for asking."

Zen was amazed to discover she had a laugh in her. Arli laughed too. "Okay, fine, why did you want to talk to me?"

"Because I've been thinking about what you said that time, about why don't I invite you, and, well, my family really is seriously weird, but . . ." Was vo actually looking bashful? "But, I was . . . What I mean is . . . would you . . . you wanna come over sometime?" They stood looking at each other. "To my dad's house, I mean. There's no easy way to have you come visit my parent I can think of."

Zen felt something loosen inside her and decided not to

be mad, at least at this one other human, in this particular moment, anymore. "All right," she said. "Thank you for the invitation."

Arli beamed. "Cool!"

"I have to ask Aunt Lucy first," Zen said.

"Okay. But you really wanna come over."

"Yeah. Sure."

"Okay, good. Good. I'll message you about . . . yes." An awkward good-bye wave, and they headed in their opposite homeward directions.

INTERLUDE: SEEING ZEN

Melissa

The cross was the first thing I noticed, actually. She has a cross on a chain around her neck, just like I do. Which, I know at least some of the other kids at school go to church, but Mom says not all that many, and of the ones that do, almost none of them would wear a cross. Not so you could see it. Mom says it's a shame that the world has come to this, and I think she's right.

Anyway, Zenobia came over to our house. I invited her, because I made the decision over the summer that I was going to try to make more friends. And we had a nice time. There was a weird thing that happened where Mom was asking questions, and Zen said both her parents were dead, and then she got all emotional, and Mom had to comfort her. That is sad, for sure. To lose both your parents so young. I wonder if she did something really bad so that God had to punish her like that.

She's not very good at word games. She got the worst score of all three of us, by about a hundred points, and after a while I could tell she was bored.

She did get weird about that other kid. The girl who thinks she's a boy. I just said what Mom said about how sad it was that some poor kid's parents would do that to her, actually encourage her like that. And Zenobia got all snappy. I did like Mom says and turned the other cheek. Still, though, I didn't understand her reaction.

I do like her, though. She really loved the bracelet I made for her, and besides that she just seems nice. I think I'm going to invite her over again.

THIRTY-THREE

THE KEDUM HOUSE was in an older neighborhood with mostly small houses, some in poor repair, some defiantly tidy. Tired fences leaned, dogs lolloping behind some. Trees with slots cut through for utility wires loomed overhead. It looked like a neighborhood where a lot of people had done a lot of hard living for a long time.

Arli's house was a beat-up old place set back from the street, with a yard full of weeds, an old pickup on blocks rusting under the car park, and a saggy roof. As Zen got out of the car, Arli's hand popped out through a sideways-levered little window—bathroom, probably—and waved. Zen said okay to Aunt Lucy, who drove away.

Arli came out onto the little concrete plinth that did for a porch. "Hey," vo said.

"Hey." Zen picked her way up the walk, which was a row of hexagonal cement tiles sunk in the grass. Arli looked un-characteristically subdued. When Zen had joined ven on the porch, vo said, "So, this is it. My little dump of a house."

"It's bigger than my old house," Zen said. "In better shape, too."

"I find that hard to believe. But thanks for saying." An awkward pause. Then, with an effort, "Okay, so, wanna come in and meet the fam? Such as they are. My dad's home, and you might even get a glimpse of my brother."

"Lester."

"That's not his real name, of course. His real name is Lynx."

"Links? You mean like, parts of a chain?"

"Or a golf course? No. L-Y-N-X. Like the animal."

"What a strange name."

"You're not wrong."

"We've had this conversation before."

"That's true."

"So what's up with that? Named after animals?"

"My parent had some odd ideas . . . um, I'll tell you another time. Dad, this is my friend Zen."

They had made their way into the living room, which was crowded with decrepit furniture, stacks of magazines, a weight set, some dirty plates here and there, and other miscellaneous grunge and clutter. Near the window a bald man with a heavy, lined face and a white cotton T-shirt sat at a little card table, busy with something. He looked up, seeming to have to work to refocus his eyes. "Hello," he mumbled.

"Hello, Mr. Kedum," said Zen. "It's nice to meet you."

Stepping forward, she saw what he was doing. He was cleaning a gun.

Mr. Kedum looked blank for a second, then said, "What was the name? Sorry, didn't catch it."

"My name is Zenobia, sir," said Zen. "Your . . . Arli calls me Zen for short." A pause. "So do other people."

"Zen. Okay, fine." Mr. Kedum's eyes shifted to Arli. "Your friend is polite."

"Yes, she is."

"And more normal than I was expecting."

Arli glowered at this, but said nothing. Zen was curious about the weapon he was cleaning. It looked familiar. "What is that?" she asked. "A Ruger?"

Arli's dad jolted slightly. "It is, yes," he said. His voice was so flat it was hard to tell, but maybe he was surprised.

Zen felt Arli's eyes on her. She flushed. "My dad had one, is all," she said. "Just like it. So I've seen one before."

Brakes squeaked outside. An engine cut off. A car door slammed. The bald man's eyes had drifted away. He turned back to the table. A sudden rat-a-tat sounded from the door, oddly precise in its rhythm. The door clonked like it had been kicked, then shuddered open. A boy came in, holding a drumstick in each hand—that explained the rat-a-tat. It was Lester, or Lynx. He had his eyes mostly closed and was grinning and head-banging to music only he could hear. He played another drum lick on the rim of a lampshade by the door. Then he saw Arli and Zen, and froze.

Everyone stared at each other for a moment. Lynx's face went red, and he snarled something without words and disappeared down the short hall that led, presumably, to bedrooms. A door slammed. After a second, the house began to shake. The manic hammering of double kick drums. The rasping scream of heavy metal vocals.

Zen looked at Arli, feeling embarrassed. From Arli's expression vo was feeling the same. After a second they both nodded. Bonding through squirm. Arli made a move with veir head toward the front door. "Come with me," vo said. "I want to show you something."

Zen gestured toward the hall. "I thought . . . your room . . ."

"It's not much to look at. And do you really want to go any deeper into that?" The music was like jackhammers.

"No, thanks."

"Come on, then."

"Where are we going?"

"You'll see."

THIRTY-FOUR

AN INITIAL STRETCH of sidewalk, and then Arli cut down a dirt path between two fenced yards. It opened into the outer reaches of a school field. By the looks of the playground, it was an elementary school. Generations of pushing feet had cut deep grooves in the ground under the swings. Tetherball poles with no tetherballs on them dotted the asphalt.

Arli led Zen around a corner into a long, narrow stretch between a blank wall on one side and a fence on the other. The ground was mostly bare dirt. Beyond the fence lay a strip of scrubby trees and bushes, then a ditch, then backyards on the other side. The green was thick enough to be hard to see through. Dogs barked and engines rumbled round about, but right where they were felt isolated and deserted.

Halfway along, a stairwell plunged into the ground next to the building. The stairs were made of rough concrete, and led down into shadow. Zen said, "What are we doing here?"

"This is the entrance to my secret place," Arli said, and started down. Zen followed, gripping the steel handrail. The air got cooler with each step. It smelled like damp cement. Grit and trash at the bottom, and a blank metal door. No keyhole in the knob, but there was one in a small round plate above.

Arli fished in veir pocket, brought out a key, and held it up with a flourish. Zen looked at the lock, at her friend. Really? Arli nodded. "Where did you get it?" she whispered. It seemed important to whisper.

"Lynx gave it to me."

"Where did he get it?"

"I don't know. He never told me."

"And he gave it to you."

"Before he got all teenagery and mean, yeah. Passing it along." Arli unlocked the door and creaked it open.

Inside, Zen was strongly reminded of the secret spaces under Lukematon. Same pipes and wires. Same low, rough ceiling. And, once Arli flipped a switch, same bare bulbs in wire cages. Arli's secret tunnels were less well lit than Zen's, though. Between the pools of glare lay long stretches of dark.

"Come on," Arli said, and they began picking their way forward. At intervals lower pipes barred the way. In a couple of places they had to crawl. They came to a T. Arli turned right and kept going. This stretch had no lights, but there was a hint of a dim-lit edge farther ahead. Another corner. One particularly glary bulb, illuminating a dead end. No, wait. There was an opening low in the wall. Zen's breath had started coming short. Virtual tunnels were fine. Real ones pressed in. But, drawn by a sense of being initiated into a ritual, she forced herself forward.

The crawl through the black square led to a new passage. It was completely dark now. Zen heard rustling in the dark, and a flashlight clicked on. "Prepared," said Arli.

"Where are we going?"

"You'll see."

Another couple of turns. They passed a ladder. "That goes up into the back of the auditorium," Arli said. "If they leave it unlocked, you can get in and climb up where the lights are."

"Going low to go high."

"Yeah."

Zen shivered. It was an oddly thrilling thought.

One last corner, and they entered a small concrete room, almost cubical. Some kind of water tank or pump or furnace took up a lot of the space, but around and under it, an underground clubhouse had been set up. Furnishings included a grotty scrap of rug, a wooden box with candles stuck to it, and two old beanbag chairs patched with duct tape. Around one, tiny foam balls littered the carpet. The air was warm and close, with tangs of mildew, wax, and smoke.

"Welcome," said Arli, "to the Fieldwork Sanctum."

"What an odd name."

"You're not wrong. Do you know why it's called that?"

Zen thought about it. "Because it's . . . hold on . . . sixteen letters with no repeats."

"Yes! You noticed! Thank you so much!"

"But what does it mean?"

"Well, obviously not what, say, an archeologist means by fieldwork. The sixteen-letters thing is the first reason, but after that, I figure fieldwork could mean something like, going somewhere and working on life stuff. So this is where I come when I need to get away and think."

"Oh. Okay." Pause. "You could call it FS for short."

"Yes, you could."

"And, check it out, FS also stands for 'for short.'"

"You know what," Arli said, smiling. "You have become a chima of words. I thought I was the only one."

"Thanks," said Zen. She looked around. "Did you bring all this stuff down here?"

"No, I didn't bring any of it. It's all been here for a long time."

"Yeah, looks like it. Smells like it too."

Arli shrugged. "It is what it is." Vo propped the flashlight against the box so that it pointed at the ceiling. Dim orange light showered down around them. Arli plumped into the wounded beanbag, and foam pellets jetted up in a plume. Vo gestured to the other beanbag. It looked none too clean, but it was too late to back out now. Zen lowered herself, and found she was almost lying on the floor. She felt something next to her hand and picked it up. It was a tattered girly magazine, so old the hairstyles looked like something on TV reruns. She made a face and tossed it away. Somewhere nearby some piece of machinery hummed, all on one droning pitch. Otherwise, silence.

Zen said, "In a weird way, it's peaceful."

"Yeah."

"I see why you come here. It's . . . secret. Safe."

"Yeah."

"A place to go where . . ."

". . . you don't have to be anything you're not."

"Right."

THIRTY-FIVE

AFTER AN INTERLUDE of quiet, Arli snagged the flashlight with an outstretched finger and started shining it different places. The shadows leapt and jittered, making Zen feel queasy, but she didn't say anything.

Arli said, "They don't get me. At all."

"Who?"

"My family. My dad and brother."

At least your parents are still alive, Zen thought, but she kept her mouth shut.

"And at school. Nobody gets me there, either. And they can get really nasty sometimes. Like there's this one group of kids, they call me . . ." Vo choked on the word, but then got it out: "'It.'"

Zen made a wordless sound of distress.

Arli looked up, scowling, and mimicked in a nasty singsong, "'Oooh, is it a boy or a girl? I can't tell! Oooh, what is it? What kind of freaky thing is it?'"

"Jeezum. I'm so sorry," Zen said. "Let me guess: Natalie."

"Among others." Arli scowled harder. "I get so mad, sometimes," vo said. "Wanting revenge." A long stare into a dark corner, then under veir breath: "I've done a few things I'm not proud of. . . ."

Despite herself, Zen felt intrigued. She knew rage. The curious places it took you. "For instance?" she asked.

Arli growled and shook veir head. "Never mind," vo said. "But you know what? You're lucky. You get to be a normal kid. Just another girl in the world. You don't know what it's like."

Zen dropped her eyes, folded one leg into the beanbag chair, and started playing with her shoelace. She yearned to say: But I do know what it's like. Once the words were out, though, there was no taking them back. And even friends could make mistakes, let something slip. The risk was too great. She couldn't say, and it just sucked so bad.

A long, uncomfortable silence, neither of them looking at the other. Zen was just starting to think it was too awkward to stay when Arli pulled a book of matches out of veir pocket and used it to light one of the candles stuck to the box. The flame rose up first sooty and weak, then yellow and strong, with hardly a flicker. Arli clicked off the flashlight and settled back into veir beanbag again.

The change of light made the room feel another layer deeper in secret. As their eyes adjusted, the warm sphere of the candle's light expanded, noiselessly pushing the gloom back until even the farthest grit-strewn corners glowed in a faint brownish illumination. The rest of the world felt apart now, and the passage of time seemed not to matter anymore—a thing that happened other places, not here. Womb space.

After another minute, Arli drew breath and spoke. "What's your number-one fandom?"

Chitchat, then. Yeah, maybe that was best for the moment. Zen said, "You first."

"That's easy," said Arli. "Novaglyph."

"Never heard of it."

"It's a web comic. Weekly updates. The artist lives in Boston, and it has a ton of trans and genderqueer characters, and it's just wicked cool. What's your number-one fandom?"

"Kimazui."

"What's that?"

"See? Nobody knows. Just like yours."

"What is it?"

"It's an anime series. It's about this team of girls with powers charged with protecting the world."

"And I bet it has girl clothes and girl hair and big shiny anime eyes and those tiny little mouths—"

"What's your point?"

"I don't know. I guess I just don't like anime very much."

"You don't have to be all judgy about it."

"Okay. Sorry."

"Okay."

Zen fiddled with her shoelace, contemplating. Her mind went to the thing that had been growing there for a couple of weeks now—the little seed of doubt that had rooted and started to sprout. To say the words would make it more real, and that was scary, but who better to talk about it with? And no safer place, no better time. After a false start or two she got the words out: "Do you believe in God?"

Arli nodded slowly. Not saying yes, just receiving the question. Vo looked her in the eyes and said, "You first."

Zen opened her mouth to object, then remembered she had just done the same thing. Okay, fine. She stared off into the gloom, gathering thoughts. "Well," she said at last, "for sure I was raised that way. Church, prayers, blessings before meals, don't take the name of the Lord in vain. All that stuff. And if you had asked me in that old life, do I believe in God, I would have said, of course I do." More thought-gathering. Then, slowly, "But, recently, I've started looking at it in a new way. Or, maybe, just looking at it, really looking, for the first time. And now . . . I'm not so sure." Words lightly spoken, but only spoken at all because they were hidden in the secret womb of light. Arli opened veir mouth as though preparing to speak, then closed it again. Zen said, making an end, "I still say my prayers, though. Habit, I guess. Your turn."

Arli mused a while, then said, "I was raised the opposite of you. Neither of my parents believed or went to church. And I've never had a reason to go against how they raised me. Especially considering how it seems like most of the people who judge in-betweeny people like me are religious people. They say stuff, I guess, like, 'God doesn't make mistakes.'" Silence.

When vo went on, veir voice had a waver in it. "I may be a lot of things, but I'm not an it, and I'm not a mistake, either."

"Of course you're not," Zen said. She smiled. "I think you're cool just the way you are."

A shaky smile in return. "Thanks. I think you're cool just the way you are too."

"Thanks." They both laughed a little. Zen said, "So I guess that takes care of that."

"Yep, all set." They laughed again.

Zen said, "So, what *do* your parents believe in?"

"Hmm . . . give me a minute."

Zen gave ven a minute. And another. Finally Arli said, "I guess my dad doesn't believe much, now that I think about it. Except that it's important to get rich. So that's what he spends all his time trying to do." The tone of Arli's voice said, Not a thing I care about, at all.

"And your . . . parent?"

Arli did a look that said, Thanks for catching that. "You remember at dinner, I talked about the Nezel traditions of gender?" Zen nodded. "If my parent believes in anything, it's that stuff. Riria Dizdi, they call it. This idea that kids ought to be able to grow up without being thought of as girls or boys until they are old enough to decide for themselves. Vo really likes that."

"There're those pronouns again."

"Yeah. For kids who haven't decided yet. Or for people like me, who have decided to stay in the middle forever."

"You've already decided about forever?"

Another eye-to-eye look. "Yeah. I have." Flat and final. Zen opened her mouth, closed it again. Arli said, "What about you? Have you ever really thought about your gender?"

Zen groped through the clanging of internal alarm bells for anything to say. At last she managed, "Not a thing I want to talk about right now."

"Why not?"

Shaky-voiced: "I just don't. For reasons I can't . . . for . . . just, reasons. Okay?" They stared at each other. With her eyes Zen begged, Please just let it go. Please.

"Okay," Arli said. "That's cool. No problem."

"Thanks," Zen whispered. And if Arli could tell how many feels there were crammed into that one word, vo gave no sign.

THIRTY-SIX

THE MIDDLE OF October. Seven weeks of school somehow survived without everything imploding. Ruminating on this miracle in Mr. Walker's first-period class one Monday, Zen didn't notice right away that Melissa was holding out a note. Mr. Walker turned toward the whiteboard and Melissa made a tiny "hey" without voice. Zen turned and saw the little square of paper. For a couple of weeks now she and Melissa had been in a sort of friend holding pattern, talking when they met, but not moving toward anything deeper. Zen had started to see in the other girl's eyes a touch of wariness she also felt herself. But there was still warmth and connection, too. She took the note.

It said: "Some Tuesdays my dad takes my brothers and little sisters out, and my mom and I do girls' night. Would you like to come tomorrow?"

Zen thought fast. The passage of time had not made what

Melissa had said—or to be precise, what she had said her mother had said—about Elijah feel any less sickening. But still, she was tempted to accept the invitation. Maybe because of seven weeks and not even one second look. Also, the roller coaster happened to be at the top of a hill. At least at this moment, she felt invincible. And she had a twisty curiosity to hear Mrs. Martin's words about Elijah from Mrs. Martin herself. Not "know your enemy," exactly, because Melissa's mom didn't feel like an enemy. Or, not just. After all, she had been kind. That hug. No, it was more wanting to hear someone actually say the words. Practice, maybe, for times that were coming.

Plus, if she could, she wouldn't mind getting another look at that brother.

The few seconds it took to work through these deliberations felt well within the allowable period for answering. On the back of the note she wrote, "I have to ask. But, yay, sounds like fun!" She added a smiley face and a flower, and passed the note back. Melissa smiled and nodded.

When, permission and a ride sought and granted, Zen showed up at the Martins' the next evening, getting another look at the brother turned out to be the first thing that happened. Talking to him too. He was sitting at the dining table doing homework, and after letting her in Melissa said, "I'm helping my mom in the kitchen," and disappeared, so it was just the two of them.

Douglas, his name turned out to be. Not Doug. Douglas.

On closer inspection he turned out to be a clean-cut and somber-looking boy. Also, formal and polite. "So, Zenobia, you're Melissa's new friend from school."

"Yes."

"I've never met someone named Zenobia before."

Zen nodded. No words.

"Is it a family name?"

Zen shook her head. She couldn't very well tell him that she had picked it out herself just a few months ago, for the Z to A of it, the feel of getting back to the beginning and starting over.

He was watching her now, maybe because he had picked up that she was answering without speaking. Zen suddenly wondered again what would happen if he, if the whole family, found out that she was like Elijah. Too late to back out now, though. Just gotta brazen it out.

"I'm named after my grandfather," Douglas said. "He was a minister."

Nod.

"We come from a long line of ministers."

Nod.

"But my dad isn't one. His brother is, though."

Zen felt the pressure of the accumulated silences and managed to say, "What's his name?"

"My dad's brother? James. Uncle Jim." Douglas closed his book and shuffled papers together in a stack. Homework done for today, looked like.

Zen thought about saying, "I have an aunt named Phil," and had to suppress a laugh. In order to have something else to say, she asked, "What about you? Do you want to be a minister too?"

The older boy seemed taken aback by the question. He stopped tidying. Their gazes met. He had gorgeous eyes. But also, now that she was looking, something . . . missing. An absence of spark. She tried to imagine him making a joke, and couldn't come up with it.

"I don't know," he said. "I guess. If I'm called." Then he went into the kitchen, where Zen heard him telling his mother that he was done, and could he go to his friend's house now? He called her *ma'am*.

At dinner, Zen listened except when answering direct questions. Her mind was full of Elijah. She groped fruitlessly for a way to bring him up . . . but then Melissa did it for her. She said to her mom, "That girl who thinks she's a boy. Remember I told you about her?"

Mrs. Martin glanced at Zen and said, "Yes, I remember."

"I saw her again today. She's still doing it. Still wearing the clothes. And using the same name."

"That's not surprising."

Astonished to hear herself speak, Zen said, "You're talking about Elijah, right?"

Melissa scoffed. "As she calls herself."

"Melissa," said her mother. "No need to mock."

Still marveling at her own boldness, Zen said, "I don't

know . . . Elijah just seems to me to be . . . just feels boy-like to me. You know? Elijah just seems to me to be Elijah."

Melissa's mom was nodding sadly. She said, "The Bible teaches us not to treat any of God's children with contempt. And it's not that poor child's fault that she's one of the gender-confused."

That was hard to take. Zen took a slow-motion sip of soda to mask her consternation.

Melissa said, "That's what you said before." She hesitated, and Zen glanced at her. Was Melissa about to say something that challenged her mother, even in a small way? Why yes, she was. "But I kind of sort of agree with Zen. She just seems like a boy to me, too. A little bit. Sometimes." Then her cheeks went red and she looked down at her plate.

Zen wondered what Mrs. Martin angry would look like. Those eyes: so warm, usually. But with those quirky corners, too. And that firm mouth. So certain. Melissa's mom mad could maybe be scary.

Tightness came into Mrs. Martin's voice. "Well, that's natural. First impressions are powerful. You met her as a boy, so in your mind she seems to be one."

Melissa nodded.

"And she's just a child." Mrs. Martin's lips had gone thin, and Zen nodded minutely to herself. Yep, something really hard there. "It's the parents I deplore," Mrs. Martin said. "That's the real shame. There's no way the situation could have gotten as far as it has without them encouraging it, or at least condoning."

"I understand now, Mother," Melissa said. "Thank you for helping me to see."

Zen felt her body start to shake. All of a sudden, this was way too close to home. Confidence evaporating. She needed to flee. "Ma'am?" she said. It came out normal-sounding, and she gave silent thanks.

"Yes, Zenobia?"

"May I use your restroom?"

"Of course, dear." A second look. "Zenobia, are you all right?"

"Yes, sorry, thanks. Um, I just, it's just that all of a sudden I have to go really bad." Already up, she performed the desperate-to-pee tiptoes dance.

"Badly."

"Yes, ma'am, badly."

"Very well. You know where, down the hall."

THIRTY-SEVEN

LATER IN OCTOBER now, with weather to match. On an afternoon cold enough for gloves, Zen came home late, just before dinnertime, to voices sounding different in the kitchen. She heard it as she eased the door shut. Like a stranger was there. And, judging from the hitchless rhythm, they hadn't heard her come in. She slipped off her shoes and whisper-walked to a spot just out of sight around the corner from the speakers.

Aunt Lucy was talking, with more than the usual edge in her voice. ". . . all this way. Everything's fine. She's doing well in school, and making friends."

The voice that answered was not Aunt Phil's, but familiar all the same. "We'll see about that." Zen's eyes widened, and she held her breath. It was Grandma Gail. Instantly Zen was transported back to the surreal dream time when she had finally made the switch.

Things had gotten so dark and strange. Still, they had

a rhythm to their days. Dad would go out and work. In the summer he did a lot of solo jobs, fixing up the winter homes of the rich people who returned once the heat broke. She was forbidden from going out. The expectation was that she was working on her homeschool lessons, but she found them easy, and they never took long. Also, he seldom checked her work. So once that was done, she spent most of her time exploring the dark web, finding solace in learning new skills, hacking new sites, designing new exploits. The rare times she tired of that, she would lie on the couch and stare endlessly out at the scrubby cactus-scattered front yard.

There had been a plan for that yard once, long ago, when Mother was still alive. Raised planters with stone wall sides. Paths between. Only remnants remained. The cacti she had planted still soldiered on, but weeds had come into the neglected dirt. Down by the river, one cottonwood tree flashed an improbably vivid swatch of green.

The weeks went by. Zen felt nothing much, most days. Locked away inside herself. Doing her time. Life without the possibility of parole.

Then the day came when he did not return. The long afternoon shaded ever so slowly into dusk, then into night, and the sound of his truck jouncing down the rutted drive failed to make itself heard.

A little waiting, and then a dive deep into herself. If there was fear it felt contained, as in a glass jar. A whole row of glass jars, actually, lined up in the cupboard of her mind, holding under their screwed-down lids all the feelings another human child might feel in this moment, so that this other thing could maybe possibly happen—a time-lapse flower maybe possibly begin to open. She waited to see if there would be enough time.

He did not return, and no one else came, and she made herself meals out of the fridge and pantry, and still he did not return, and no one else came. Her father, her last living parent, had disappeared, and she existed alone in their little patch of desert that grew hotter every day. Alone with the smell of scorched dust and the wind-rattle hush and the glare of the sunlight through the long afternoons.

She had long ago marked the location of the boxes in her mind. She knew exactly which shelf they rested on, out in the shed. On the morning of the fourth day she rose, ate cereal with canned milk and raisins, and then stepped out into the tuning-up-to-furnace morning and walked the stone path to the shed and pulled the boxes down.

And when, a day later, Thomas Jarecky's absence having finally been noted somewhere out in the world, Grandma Gail showed up and peeked through the blinds, she saw her grandchild in the living room, wearing one of her mother's faded housedresses and dancing—to an old swing record—an ecstatic couch-leaping, arm-flinging, lamp-tipping, ululating dance.

To say the least, Grandma Gail was less than pleased with what she found. When, another day later, Zen's father was found dead in a wash with a rifle bullet in his skull, Zen trembled under that hard gaze, afraid of another cycle of the rigid God-words that had clamped her life out of the world until now.

Somehow, though, that didn't happen.

Grandma Gail was not one to ask a grandchild what that grandchild wanted, but she did seem to have a different sort of relationship with God than Father and Mother had had. One with a little more wiggle room in it. And Grandma did have two children, though eldest Lucille lived so far away and was in contact so seldom. When Lucille came to the memorial service and heard what had happened, a conversation had begun. Out of that conversation, an offer of guardianship had been made. And now, many months later, Zen stood in a hallway a thousand miles from the nearest natural-growing cactus or cottonwood tree, listening to her relatives talk about her.

THIRTY-EIGHT

"I'M GLAD TO hear you think the child is doing well," Grandma Gail said. She didn't sound glad. "But, if you don't mind, I am also going to want to see and hear for myself."

Aunt Lucy said, "And anyway, there's nothing you can do about it. I am her legal guardian now. It's done. It's official. You can give me as many of your looks as you like, but—"

Aunt Phil's voice cut in. "Ms. Jarecky, are you sure I can't supply you with some refreshment? While we wait for the young one to appear? Should be any minute now."

"Oh, all right, if you insist. A glass of ice water." Zen heard Aunt Phil stand and walk across the floor. A cupboard opened and shut. The loose floorboard in front of the fridge creaked. The freezer opened. A hand scrabbled among half-moons in their tray. Ice clinked musically into a glass. Grandma's voice said, "I will say that I do like what you've done with this place. Seems real cozy."

"Thank you," said Aunt Lucy in a cold voice.

"And the dresses and such . . . is he still persisting in that?" Zen had been expecting the male pronoun, but it still hurt when it came. She clenched her teeth and concentrated on breathing soundlessly.

There was a heavy silence. Then Aunt Lucy said even more frostily, "*She* is enjoying herself, as far as we can tell, dressing in new clothes that were acquired for her for school."

"What sort of clothes?"

"Natural clothes such as any girl would wear."

Grandma Gail made a scornful sound. Aunt Phil cut in again. "Will you be staying for dinner, Ms. Jarecky?"

"No, I have plans. I actually have a friend in this city, believe it or not. Or in Boston, anyway. She's driving up. I'm not a total rube who's never been out of her little patch of Arizona, you know."

Aunt Phil said soothingly, "No, of course not."

Zen risked discovery every moment she remained in the hallway, and she had heard enough. She tiptoed back to the front door, eased it open, slipped through, and closed it softly behind her.

On the porch she drew a shaky breath and blew it out again. Some acting required now. But she saw the way it would go. Another breath, in, out. Then, hand on the doorknob. Not too much now, just enough. She rattled as she turned, let the door bang against its stop. "Hey!" she called down the hall. She had done this before, other days. All in the bounds of normal. "I'm home!" Realizing she was barefoot, she hastily acted out pushing off her shoes.

"Tweetie-bird!" called Aunt Phil from the kitchen.

"Whose car is in the driveway?" Zen called back.

Aunt Lucy came into view, stopping where Zen had stood seconds before. Her face was tight and angry. "Zenobia, come into the kitchen," she said. "We have a visitor."

Zen put on her best expectant/curious face and followed her aunt's beckoning hand. Rounding the corner, she did an artfully natural double take. Then, "Grandma!" Mostly surprise, plus a hint of happiness to see her. Genuine happiness. After all, she was a good grandma in her way. Just set in her mind about some things. The meanings, for instance, of the words "boy" and "girl."

"Hmph," said Grandma Gail, staring, and Zen's face went hot. She looked down at her dress, smoothed it. Then she made her eyes come back up to meet the grandmaternal laser beams. "Well," Grandma Gail said, and then she said Zen's old boy name. "Still at it, I see."

Zen trembled on the edge of looking down again, but kept herself from doing it. Her face got hotter. Her heart tocked in her ears. "My name," she said, "is not that, what you said, anymore."

"The name your parents gave you."

"My name is Zen now. Zenobia. Zenobia July."

Grandma Gail's already sharp tone got even sharper. "You don't even intend to keep your family name?"

Aunt Lucy cut in. "In point of fact," she growled, "it's already done. We started the name-change process shortly after Zen moved in, and it went through mid-summer." Zapping tension between Aunt Lucy and Grandma Gail now. Possible explosion building.

"That's the reason for 'July,'" said Aunt Phil, in her mild pixie-smiling way. "Same initial, and the month it went through."

Zen nodded. "That's right." Grandma Gail turned the laser beams back on her, but Zen, checking the Aunties' faces and seeing little nods, lifted her chin and looked steadily back. "Plus, I just like it."

Zen moved around to Aunt Phil and leaned against her. A protective and comforting arm curled around. Aunt Lucy stepped over too and put a hand on Zen's shoulder. All three together they faced their matriarch.

Grandma Gail's mouth worked. But, slowly, her glinting gaze dimmed, then wobbled away. The silence stretched. Over her head, Zen saw the Aunties exchange a look. What was happening?

At last Grandma Gail looked up again. Her face had changed. She was a woman, they all three knew, hardened by a hard life, and unused to opposition to her will. Also, usually, immune to self-doubt. That emotion, though, was now written plainly on her face.

Her voice when she spoke was softer, a touch wavery. "God knows it's a strange world, isn't it?" she said. "And sometimes it's good to remember that to assume that you know everything about anything risks the sin of pride." She looked Zen in the face again, a searching look. "D— I mean, uh, child, uh, Zen . . ." She paused and whispered to herself, "Zen. Zen. Zenobia." Then, "So, this is truly what you want?"

Zen was nodding vehemently, and her answer burst out over the end of the question: "Oh yes, so much. I really am just a girl. I mean, I know, the body I was born with is a boy body. But this just feels so good, so right. So . . ." She waved her hands in the air, unable to find the word. "It's just . . . me. This is me. I'm me!" Aunt Phil squeezed her at the same time that Aunt Lucy pressed her shoulder. Zen kept her face up, and watched her grandmother work.

At last Grandma Gail said, "Well, I don't pretend to understand. I do think that it is contrary to God's law." Her eyes shifted to Aunt Lucy. "But there you are, still my child. In spite of your lifestyle."

Aunt Lucy twitched at the word *lifestyle*, but said, with new gentleness, "Yes, here I am. Still your child."

Grandma Gail looked back at Zen. "And there you are, still my grandchild. And you seem happy."

A long silence. Aunt Phil broke it by saying, "Are you sure you won't stay? Even for a little while?"

Grandma Gail shook her head and pushed herself to standing. Zen was startled to see that her grandmother looked more bent than just a few months ago. The old woman began to shuffle toward the front door. Close to Zen she stopped and stared at her one more time. Zen broke from the Aunties' grasps and hugged her. "I love you, Grandma," she said.

"Hmph." But a grandmotherly hand patted twice on Zen's back. "Now, I am going."

At the door, Grandma Gail submitted stiffly to a dutiful kiss on the cheek from Aunt Lucy. The last thing she said was to Zen: "I would never have believed it if I hadn't seen it with my own eyes. You actually look pretty, child." And she was gone, leaving her granddaughter breathless and glowing in the doorway.

THIRTY-NINE

TWENTY MINUTES LATER, just as they sat down to dinner, the doorbell rang. Looks went around the table, and Zen saw that the two adults were thinking the same thing she was: that Grandma Gail had changed her mind and had come back to say so. Aunt Lucy frowned and went down the hall to the front door. Zen followed, chewing her lip. Aunt Lucy pressed the intercom button. "Hello?"

"Darling!" cried a voice, and Zen closed her eyes and said a silent thanks. It was Uncle Sprink.

He had come to deliver signs. The Aunties and their friends did a lot of marching and waving signs and gathering to hear each other give speeches. Aunt Lucy liked to mention the number of times she had been arrested: five. To Zen it seemed an absurd thing to be proud of. In the first weeks living in the house she had politely but firmly declined several invitations to march and wave signs with them, and then had pushed back against some actual pressure, until they had finally gotten the message. *So not interested.*

Uncle Sprink declined to join them for dinner, saying he had more signs to deliver, but he did linger for a little while to talk. Munching her stir-fry, working around the tofu cubes, Zen studied his face. There was something unusual about it. It took a minute, but then she saw it: his eyebrows were thin. Since Natalie's comment, Zen had been noticing eyebrows. All the men she had looked at had thick, bushy ones. Mr. Walker, for instance. But Uncle Sprink's were two high, thin arcs, no more than a few hairs wide.

Their guest noticed that she was staring and gave her a smile. Zen forced herself to speak. "Uncle Sprink, may I ask you a question?"

"Of course."

"Okay, um . . . there was a thing at school . . . someone said something . . . and now, some kids, they're doing this finger-waggling thing when they see me . . . um, do you think my eyebrows are too thick?"

"Your eyebrows are beautiful just the way they are," said Aunt Lucy firmly, but she wasn't even looking. Uncle Sprink was. Zen made herself return his gaze.

"Of course they're gorgeous just the way they are," he said. "But, if, say, for instance, a girl wanted her eyes to, you know, pop a little bit more, she could use tweezers to pull a few hairs here and there and, you know, do a little shaping."

The thought made Zen cringe. Hair plucking definitely came under the no-body-mod squidginess umbrella. She rubbed her finger over her eyebrows. The hairs crunched slightly.

"And a girl doing such a thing, she would probably do well to start working her way up from the bottom, rather than down from the top. The more space around your eyes, the more lovely they appear. Does that make sense?"

"Yes, thank you." And then he was saying good-bye.

Later, on a Cyberlandium break, Zen found herself crunching her eyebrows again. She picked up her phone and checked her reflection. Too dim to see. Her mouth grinched tight, and she got up and slipped out the door. Aunt Lucy was typing intently on a laptop at the kitchen table and did not notice her. Aunt Phil was at work.

Down the short hall to the bathroom. Light on. Push through the mirror squirm. She studied her eyebrows in the glass.

They were grotesque, she saw now. Huge, bristly, hideous black caterpillars of hair.

So, tweezers. That was what Uncle Sprink had said.

She stared herself in the eyes a bit more, working up nerve. Most people, she supposed, would have no problem with a simple thing like plucking hairs. But she wasn't most people. Still, she had to try.

She fetched the tweezers from the medicine cabinet, then leaned close to the mirror, angling to get good light from above.

She zeroed in on the lower edge of her right eyebrow. There was one hair there that drooped down out of line with the others. Her hand trembling slightly, she pinched the tweezer-jaws closed around it. The hair felt tough and fibrous through the metal. She tugged. The skin pulled up in a little chocolate-kiss shape, but the hair remained fixed. "Ow!" she said. The pain was pointed and tickly at the same time. She scrubbed at the place to make the tickle go away.

Take two. Teeth clenched, she clamped again, took a breath, held it, and yanked. The hair plocked free. It hurt a lot for a single hair. Zen made a grinding noise in her throat.

She examined the place the hair had come from. Tiny red dot. She scrubbed again to erase the tickle. She examined the hair, still death-gripped in the tweezers. It had a little bulby bit on the end with what looked like a tiny drop of milky liquid surrounding it. Suddenly she felt repulsed. She gagged, wrapped the hair in a square of toilet paper, flushed it, dropped the tweezers back in the cabinet, and scurried to her room.

So, yeah, God.

I am so Goddamnittohell tired. And, yeah, name in vain. I did it on purpose.

I'm just so weary. I am weary of life.

And I just totally heard Grandma Gail in my head say, You're only a child. You are too young to be weary of life.

To which I answer her, answer everyone, answer you: Don't ever tell me what I'm too young to be.

What Melissa's mom said. "Gender confused." That really got to me.

I am not confused.

When I put that dress on, Mom's dress: I felt something I had never felt before. I felt like for the first time in my life someone had put their arms around me and was telling me I was going to be okay. You know, the words moms say.

It's okay, baby.

I'm here.

I've got you.

Shhh, honey, it's going to be all right.

I love you just the way you are, and I always will.

Damn it, I've already cried so much. I'm sick of crying.

What I wouldn't give to hear my mother saying those words to me now. Because she was a good mom.

She used to sing to me. She loved those old-time songs. The hymns, but also the silly nursery rhyme songs. Like,

> *Down in the meadow*
> *In a sly little den*
> *Lived an old mother spider*
> *And her little spiders ten*
> *"Spin!" said the mother*
> *"We spin!" said the ten*
> *And they spun and were glad*
> *In their sly little den.*

And once we were playing one of those little kid board games, Snakes and Ladders, and I almost won, but then I hit the big snake just a few squares from the win box and I had to slide all the way back down to the first row, and I cried, and if Dad had been there he would have told me to be a man about it, but Mom didn't say that. She just held me and said those words moms say.

She let me cry.

She let me feel my feels, and didn't make me feel bad about them.

It's like she almost saw me.

Not really. But, a little.

And, I guess? I guess . . .

I guess that's all I ever get.

INTERLUDE: SEEING ZEN

Grandma Gail

His mother was a godly woman. It was sad when she died so young. Some particularly nasty tumor. She was gone in six months.

The boy took his mother's death real hard. Devastated, not too strong a word. And it went on and on. The crying and the moping, and then stomping fits of rage, and then more crying. His father kept telling him to be a man, and he just kept crying.

There always was something off about that boy. A little wisp of a kid, and so clingy, always just wanting to hang out with his mother. And, oh my God, what a soft heart. I remember once I was driving him, coming home from something after dark, and I hit a rabbit in the road—no chance to swerve, it was there and then bumpity-bump, just like that—and he asked what the sound was, and when I told him, well, he just started to bawl. "Poor little bunny," he kept saying. "Poor little bunny." And him maybe, what, eight years old by then? Two, three years after his mother's death. Pathetic, is what it was. No toughness to him. Not a proper boy at all.

And then the thing with the clothes. I still don't know what to make of that. Finding him like that, all dressed up and dancing. And that wasn't the first time. We put it down to childish play before, when he was little. We thought he was just messing around with his mother's things. But I guess it was there, whatever it is, all along. He's living as a girl now, out there with Lucille. Seems unnatural to me. But I thought about it, and I decided to leave well enough alone. When I was younger, I might have gone in there and thrown my weight around, but now . . . well, the kid seems happy. Or at least, if not happy, more . . . natural. Something like that. And who am I to judge?

FORTY

NOT NEARLY ENOUGH sleep. So hard to break through the membrane and face another day. It was Aunt Phil who finally rousted her out, ignoring her snarls and even a flailing fist, nudging and nudging with unfazeable good humor until Zen got up just to make it stop. And then there were fresh doughnuts from the little doughnut shop at the bottom of the hill to go with the usual healthier fruits and grains, and that was enough to get Zen out the door. Despite the dark tunnel the roller coaster had entered today.

As she approached school she saw Clem coming from the other direction, across the bridge over the highway. He waved, and when they were close enough to talk he said, "Did you hear? The hacker struck again last night."

For the first time since waking, Zen felt something like a spark. "Really?"

"Yeah."

"More anti-Muslim stuff?"

"I don't know. I haven't heard."

"Okay, cool."

Clem looked puzzled. "You think it's cool?"

"No, I'm sorry. It's just, maybe my tracker worked. I gotta go." And despite it being ten minutes before the bell, Zen hurried to Mr. Walker's room.

When she arrived, Mr. Walker wasn't there, but Robert was. She didn't think to scope first, and there they were, the only two people in the room. The boy looked up and scowled. "You again," he said.

"Is Mr. Walker around?" One hopeless try to keep it normal.

"He was, but he went to the office."

"Oh."

A crackling, mega-awkward silence. Zen kept her eyes down, but she knew she was being stared at. When Robert spoke again his tone was carefully light. Underneath, though, she could hear the whisper of the sword being pulled from its sheath. "So, you a gamer?"

"Sometimes."

"You seem to know an awful lot."

"I don't know what you mean."

"Right." Zen risked a glance. He was still staring. "Like, Lukematon. And mice." Tone still light, but this was all-out battle now.

"I don't know what you're talking about."

"That's a lie."

Zen had started to shake. Eye contact now. "Take that back."

"Who *are* you?" They glared at each other. "You are so weird. It's like, you're not like a regular girl at all. It's like, you're putting on an act."

Zen felt tumbled over as though by a giant wave. Disaster. There was no good way forward. Was she about to speak? Her mouth opened, probably to say something she would regret saying for the rest of her life. And at that moment, Mr. Walker reentered the room.

Zen felt herself lurch back into her body. The teacher's return had instantly rewritten the rules of combat. She saw in Robert's face that he thought the same. The showdown was going to have to happen—no avoiding it—but maybe not right now. Right now would be so terrible in so many ways. Robert's eyes faltered. He glanced at the clock, then turned and bustled out of the room, making a show of heading to the bathroom before class.

"Zen," said Mr. Walker, looking at her expectantly. "Have you heard? We had another hack last night."

Straining as hard as she could toward a normal face and voice, she stammered, "Oh, y-yes? Um . . . okay?"

"And this time, whoever it was changed all the passwords on the site, so we had a harder time shutting it down. The hack was up until about an hour ago. We had to contact the company."

Despite still reeling from the encounter with Robert, Zen

felt a touch of interest. Not super-subtle, that, but a cute finesse. She could hardly say that out loud, though. Instead she said, "And the tracker?"

"It worked. We got the IP address."

"May I see it?"

Mr. Walker blinked at this. Maybe he had been expecting more of a pleased reaction? Looking for a little yay? Instead of this weird intensity.

Zen watched as he pulled a file folder out of his briefcase. She stepped close. There was a yellow sticky note on the front of the folder with the distinctive dot-separated number clusters of an IP address written on it in neat pen. Mr. Walker looked down at it, then up again. Sounding hesitant, he said, "What good would that do? I mean, at this point, it's for the authorities to handle, wouldn't that be right?" And he moved the folder back toward the briefcase.

"Yes, sir," Zen said. In the five seconds it had been visible, she had memorized the sequence of numbers. To move him past the moment, she asked, "Was it more anti-Muslim memes?"

"No. This time it was anti-transgender."

Zen staggered. A high buzz started in her ears. She opened her mouth. She had no idea what she was going to say. Words came out. "I know who the hacker is."

"Really? Who?"

"Robert."

"What? Robert? Robert Grant?" Upon these words, the

boy himself, as if on cue, came back into the room. "Are you sure, Zenobia? That's a very serious accusation."

Zen looked at the hated rival who had just said that her girlhood was an act. "I'm sure," she said. "He's the hacker. I have proof."

Robert gaped, eyes first puzzled, then switching over to blazing. Mr. Walker, looking troubled, said, "All right, then, I guess we need to go talk to some people. Robert? Would you please come with me? And, Zenobia, you had better come too."

It ended up being Robert in front, Mr. Walker in the middle, and Zen behind, walking three in a line down to the office. Zen kept her head down, to avoid the blaster eyes Robert kept shooting back, but also because of the whirlwind of feels buffeting inside her. She had big trouble now. Because, all the rage in the world, plus a strong feeling . . . Well, a few seconds ago, it had felt like certainty. So she had said what she had said. Including the part about proof.

But, in fact, she had no proof at all.

FORTY-ONE

SITTING IN THE outer office, waiting for Aunt Lucy to show up, Zen squirmed. What do you do after you jump off a cliff? Not much else to do but fall. And wait to hit the bottom. One tiny bright spot—after saying what he had to say, Mr. Walker excused himself to return to teaching. So at least the one teacher she actually liked would only hear about her humiliation later, instead of witnessing it firsthand.

After a stretch of time that seemed simultaneously too long and not nearly long enough, Aunt Lucy arrived. Thunder was brewing in her face. "What is this about, Zenobia?" she said.

Zen could only work her mouth soundlessly and blush.

"Are you in trouble?"

"I . . . I can't explain."

"Please try."

To Zen's at least momentary relief, the receptionist cut in.

"Excuse me," he said. "Assistant Principal Bowen will see you now."

Assistant Principal Nettie Bowen (said the plaque on her desk) turned out to be a brisk, businesslike woman who seemed the sort to stand for no nonsense. While the two adults said courteous things, Zen scrunched herself into the farthest corner of the farthest chair. Aunt Lucy sat down in the next chair and said, "Now, will someone please tell me what this is about?"

Ms. Bowen gave Zen a look combining pursed lips and raised eyebrows: Well? Zen blushed again and stared at the floor. Ms. Bowen said, "All right, then, I'll say it. Someone has to. Zenobia has accused another student, Robert Grant, of being the person behind a couple of recent security breaches on the Monarch Middle School website. Mr. Walker, who teaches both children in first period, reports that she has said she has proof."

Here it was. The moment of impossible quandary. The moment of no good next moment. Assistant Principal Bowen turned to Zenobia again and said, "Zenobia, is this true?"

Zenobia kept staring at the floor. Her face felt like a balloon full of hot blood, ready to burst.

"Zenobia. You have made a serious accusation. Is it true, what you said?"

A flare of sudden, desperate anger. "He had access to Mr. Walker's laptop! He had worked on it before! He got mean when he heard about the tracker. The new memes are . . .

um . . . never mind that part. But it's obvious, he's the only one who could have gotten the password." Aunt Lucy put a hand on her shoulder, and Zen fell silent.

Leaning forward in her chair, Ms. Bowen said, "Zenobia, please look at me."

Reluctantly, Zen brought her face up.

Ms. Bowen said, "Sometimes, when we are angry, we say things we don't mean." Zen flushed hard red yet again. "And from what you said a moment ago, I can see how a person might suspect that Robert had something to do with what happened on the school's website. But suspicion is one thing, and proof is another. So I'm going to ask you again: Do you in fact have proof that Robert Grant is the hacker?"

Looong silence. Aunt Lucy's hand squeezed Zen's shoulder, but Zen couldn't tell what it meant. The anger drained out of her. She slumped in her chair. At last, she mumbled, "No, ma'am."

Aunt Lucy's hand went away, and inside, Zen plunged down toward blackness. The two adults were still talking, but she paid no attention. She had ruined her life, but at least the ordeal was over. She would just stop coming to school, and she would never have to deal with Robert ever again.

Wrong. Robert was in the front office, with two people who could only be his parents, a man and a woman, both wearing business clothes and looking affronted. "That's her," Robert said when he saw Zen.

The man stepped forward. Aunt Lucy stepped forward

too, meeting him toe to toe. Neither offered a hand. In a loud, belligerent voice, the man said, "Are you this girl's mother?"

Aunt Lucy's voice was quieter, but steely. "Her guardian."

"And she accused my son, Robert, of sabotaging the school website?"

"Yes, she did." Aunt Lucy took a breath to continue, but Mr. Grant rode over her.

"Well then," he said. "In that case, what I want to know now is, what sort of restitution is going to be made for this unjust accusation? Against my son? This . . . this slander?"

"Restitution?"

"This girl has made a public accusation against my son. She is liable for damages."

Still icily polite, Aunt Lucy said, "Excuse me. Not public."

"What?"

"Respectfully, the accusation was not public. It was made in confidence to a teacher, and other than that teacher and Assistant Principal Bowen, we here are the only ones who know about it."

"That makes no difference. This is totally unacceptable."

"Also, before you interrupted me," Aunt Lucy continued, "I was going to add that, under questioning just now, Zenobia retracted her accusation."

Zen couldn't help glancing at Robert, seeing the instant victory sneer she expected. "Ha!" he said. "You don't know what you're talking about, you freak!"

"That's a laugh!" Zen snarled. "You don't know what *you're* talking about, you pathetic noob!"

"Zenobia!" Aunt Lucy said, and Zen subsided, face burning.

Robert's father's face was still heavy with anger. Aunt Lucy said in a steady, measured tone: "Mr. Grant, I suggest that if you take a moment to think about it, you'll see that the matter is resolved." Mrs. Grant put a hand on her husband's arm, as if to say, Let's just get out of here. "However," Aunt Lucy continued, "if you feel compelled to lawyer up and press the point, you can rest assured that as Zen's legal guardian, I am prepared to spare no expense in fighting back every inch of the way. And I do know some excellent attorneys." Mr. Grant's eyes wavered, just a little. Aunt Lucy's voice was even softer as she added, "And if you do choose to proceed, I'd also suggest first making certain that Zenobia's accusation was in fact unfounded. Just because she doesn't have proof doesn't mean she is wrong."

Robert turned white. Mr. Grant looked at his son, and for a second doubt was plain in the paternal face. The Grant parents exchanged a look, and then Mr. Grant said huffily, "I find that to be highly unlikely." The force had gone out of his voice, though. And then the Grant parents harrumphed their way out the door, taking Robert with them.

In the hall, Aunt Lucy steered Zen to an out-of-the-way bench. She said, "Zen, what got into you?"

Zen shook her head. How could she possibly put into words the tangled ball of rage, hurt, and fear that still careened around inside her? "I'm sorry, Aunt Lucy," she managed at last. "Are you mad at me?"

"Yes, I'm mad at you," said Aunt Lucy bluntly. Raised by an unpredictably explosive father, Zen quailed. She was startled by what Aunt Lucy said next. "But it's all right. People can be mad at each other and still have it be okay." They can? "And," Aunt Lucy went on, "that's not the strongest feeling I'm feeling. My strongest feeling right now is concern. You are under an enormous amount of pressure, and I'm not certain how to help you."

Zen gasped, so strong was the sudden uprush of feelings inside her. "Oh, but you are," she said fervently. "You are helping so much. You and Aunt Phil both. I wouldn't even be able to go to school or do anything except for how much you've helped me." Aunt Lucy had a hand up to her mouth—an unusual move for her. "So, thank you. Thank you with all my heart."

Aunt Lucy was not nearly as touchy-lovey as Aunt Phil, but when Zen suddenly lurched forward and wrapped her arms around her, she squeezed back. "You're welcome," she said. They held each other for a few more seconds, disengaged. Aunt Lucy said, "Do you want to spend the rest of the day at home?"

"Yes, please."

"All right, then. Let's go home."

FORTY-TWO

FRIDAY MORNING THERE was no way Zen was going into that first-period classroom, but once it was safely too late to have to figure out how to face Robert and Mr. Walker, she began to think maybe she could swing the rest of the day. After yesterday, how could things possibly get worse? So she asked Aunt Lucy to write her a tardy note, and went.

Things got worse.

It started toward the end of third period. Giggles in the back of the room. She sneaked a look and saw two heads bent over a phone. Ms. Owen particularly hated phones in class and barked a command. All heads turned, and Zen felt a hollow feeling in her stomach. The two laughing faces had both looked right at her. Kids she didn't even know.

In the hall after class, it seemed like every hand had a phone in it, and every face had a smirk on it. And were all eyes on her? She was so used to the squirmy feeling that they were, it was hard to separate this out. But as she approached the cafeteria, she grew more certain. Something was out there on all those little screens. Something about her.

In a trance of building horror she robot-walked the food court. Her steps slowed as she approached the archway into the eating area. She took a deep breath and held it. This was going to suck so hard she would probably die. She rounded the corner.

No doubt about it. Eyes everywhere. Sneaky, mocking, gleeful eyes. A gust of giggle moved around the room, flitting from table to table. Zen felt dizzy. She locked her gaze on the orphan misfits' table. Only Clem was there. He looked at her with an expression full of pain and sympathy. Feeling like she might pass out, she robot-walked toward him.

Suddenly a face rose up in front of her. A face with wire-frame glasses. She stopped. It was the boy Paul. He said, "I think your eyebrows are nice." Which was, she supposed distantly, sweet of him. And brave, to say so in front of the mocking multitude. She gave him a blank nod and stepped around. So, something about eyebrows. What a surprise.

As she sat down she heard the word *caterpillars*. She looked at Clem. "How bad is it?" she said.

Clem looked miserable. "Bad."

"Who has it?"

Clem just shook his head.

"Everyone?"

"Gone viral, pretty much."

Zen felt the room tilt. She clutched the table for support. "Show me."

Clem winced. "You don't have to," he said. "Why? You don't have to look."

"Yes. Yes I do. I have to know."

Clem was not taking out his phone, so Zen took hers out instead. Access, search. And there it was.

It was actually quite clever. Even in the depths of her life-ending mortification, she could see that it was clever.

Someone had made a gif. It was a picture of her face. The second picture that girl Olive had taken, zoomed in so much it had a grainy look. Only a bit of her nose, her eyes, her eyebrows, and some of her hair in the frame. And someone had animated in little feelers and googly eyes on both eyebrows. The feelers twitched back and forth each time the gif played. The googly eyes googled, rolling around and back. Caterpillar eyebrows. So very clever.

Zen took one last look around the room. Openly mocking faces now. Actual pointing and laughing. Her face, she sensed, must be bone white. But, really, in a way, she felt nothing. A sort of protective numbness had taken hold. If she could feel, it would kill her. So, the merciful numb.

Zen stood up. She shook off Clem's hand. Leaving her lunch tray on the table, she lifted her head high and started walking toward the exit doors. Not the ones back into the school. The ones with the metal grills in the windows and the alarmed crash bar that led outside. Laughter swelled. Zen was trembling. The tears pressed up behind her eyes. She began to walk faster. She would not cry in front of them. She refused to let them see that. She began to run. She hit the crash bar. The alarm blared, instant and deafening. A teacher voice shouted in surprise.

The door scraped rustily open, and she was out into the cold air. Two teacher voices behind her now, calling query and alarm. She began to run. She rounded the corner to the front of the school. Footsteps behind, falling back. Big, lumbering someone, unable to keep up. No cars coming in either direction, so she angled across the street, still running. She cut back under the trees and into the park.

It felt good to be running. She would go home. She would go into her room. She would lock the door. Whatever the Aunties might say or do wouldn't matter, because she was done. Nowhere left to go now but back to the only place she had ever felt truly safe and in control of her life and self. Back to the secret dark under-halls and haunts of Cyberlandium. Back where she knew herself best, powerful and free.

As she approached the apartment house steps, her phone rang. Zen glanced at the screen. Aunt Lucy. She pulled up short. Right, she had barged out in the middle of the day. Of course the school had contacted her guardian. Zen stared at the phone in her hand, debating whether to answer. Just before it was about to go to voice mail she snarled a swear word and tapped the screen. "Aunt Lucy," she said flatly.

"Zenobia? Are you all right? I just got a call from the school."

Zen groped for a tale to tell, and then, finding none, decided to go with the truth, whatever the consequences. "I freaked out," she said. "Some kids were teasing me, and all of a sudden I couldn't take it anymore, so I left."

Silence on the other end of the line. Zen used her last shred of patience with other humans to restrain herself from saying more. At length Aunt Lucy said, "I see. But you're okay?"

"Yes, I'm fine. Just done with school for today." More silence. "Okay? I'll just go home?" Another pause. Zen made a final effort to at least sound like she was still playing by the rules. "And try again next week?"

One last pause. Then Aunt Lucy said, "All right. Very well. I'll call them back and tell them it's okay."

Zen nodded curtly, once. "Thank you."

"You're welcome."

Knowing it was abrupt, but so needing to be done, Zen ended the call.

FORTY-THREE

THE APARTMENT WAS empty when she arrived. She slammed through to the bathroom, closed and locked the door, splashed her tear-blubbered face, then sat down on the toilet with her fingers knotted between her knees and worked to slow her breathing. She was hot from the run home, and presently it seemed to her that her self had a smell it hadn't had before. Like boys standing too close in line.

She sniffed her underarm. There was a pong. Definitely. Her face twisted. No! No no no. Please please, not that on top of everything else. Now: so not the time. The worst possible time. This was outrage piled on outrage, insupportable.

And yet, as her breathing gentled, she sensed something still unsnapped inside. She could feel it there, thrumming—a wire-tight thread of refusing to give up just yet.

Why hadn't it snapped?

It just hadn't. She didn't know why. Somehow, though, she still had strength.

Enough to face the face in the mirror?

Only one way to find out.

She turned on both lights, the overhead and the one above the sink. She turned toward the mirror with her eyes closed. She inhaled and exhaled two deep breaths. She opened her eyes.

Boy face. Boy boy boy. Which was what she had been expecting. Still, her heart shriveled. She forced herself to keep looking anyway.

Bones: wrong. Skull: too big. Jaw: too heavy. Her fingers probed her neck. Was her Adam's apple starting to grow? Today, it seemed yes. And was that the start of heavier hairs on her upper lip? Was some of the peach fuzz thickening, darkening? She wished for more light. She wished for the spotlight glare of certain truth.

Avoiding the worst as long as she could, she ran her fingers through her hair. That at least grew thick and strong, and was getting longer. The longest points bent their tips gently on her shoulders now. She lifted her chin, tilted her head . . . and, just for a second, her face flashed girl. She gasped, but when she moved her mouth, her jaw looked heavy again.

And, despite the endless, massive squirm, she couldn't not look anymore. Time to face the worst.

She stared at her eyebrows.

Monstrous, hideous. Great bushy blobs of coarse black hair, splatted like a couple of roadkill raccoons above her eyes.

She pinched them with both hands and tugged. Her skin

pulled out. She jerked them up and down. The hairs felt like steel cables under her finger pads.

The tweezers had been so bad, before. That little white drop around the bulb of the hair. What had it been? Pus? What was that other word? Lymph? Zen retched. She so did not care to know about body insides. If only you could be a perfect shell on the outside, and a mysterious miracle everywhere underneath.

But there were no longer any other options. The tweezers it had to be.

She fetched them. Leaning close, she studied her eyebrows minutely in the mirror. There were a few dark hairs between them. All right, those would do for a start. She pinched a big one right in the middle. Remembering how, the first time, not pulling hard enough had hurt more, she steeled her muscles, clenched her teeth, and yanked with her whole arm. A "huh!" escaped her lips.

It hardly hurt at all. She examined the tip of the tweezers. One curved black lash. Thicker on one end, tapering to invisibility at the other. No white blob.

Not so bad?

Not so bad.

Shaking the hair off into the wastepaper basket didn't work. She had to brush it loose from the tweezers, and then it drifted sideways and hung on the plastic liner. She growled at it, thought a moment, then tore off a single square of toilet paper.

She tweezed another hair, then pinched it out of the tweezers with the toilet paper. Repeat. Repeat. The stings of the yanks built to a hard tickle, so every few hairs she paused to rub the tickle away. Soon the skin between her eyes had no hairs darker than fuzz in it.

Which only made the dark furry brows look that much more appalling.

Now that she was looking closely, she could see that part of the bushiness came from stray hairs that straggled above and below the main swath of close-together hairs. She set to work on them, under the brows first. The skin just above her eyes was looser, so the yanks hurt more again, making her eyes water. But she was indifferent to the pain now. Not numb. It still hurt. Just finally accepting that there was no way around it. It simply had to be endured.

The problem was, every hair removed made the remaining ones look bigger, darker. Branches. Tree trunks. She had twin forests of vile ugliness growing on her face. She leaned closer, breathing now through her mouth. She began switching back and forth, left right left right, trying to get them balanced.

She couldn't get them balanced.

She couldn't get the shapes right.

But there was momentum now. Her mind switched into a half dream familiar from Cyberlandium-time. Back and forth. Thinning, thinning.

Time went a little wonky. Sense of self, likewise, slipped

out of focus. Then she stepped back from the mirror with a sharp in-hiss of breath. She had run out of hairs to pluck. The skin above her eyes was completely hairless, marked now only by twin slashes of angry red skin.

Zen opened her mouth to scream. But, no. Neighbors all around. No one must hear or see, no one must know. She swallowed the scream and, instead, made a fist and swung it down toward the glass. Whack! The bottles and other things inside the medicine cabinet rattled on their shelves. Luckily, the glass did not break.

Zen flung the tweezers rattling into the bathtub, whirled, yanked the door open, lunged across the kitchen into her room, and slammed and locked the door behind her.

FORTY-FOUR

A STRETCH OF black time. What pulled her past it: the call of Cyberlandium, waxing stronger again. She got up off the bed and opened her laptop. She felt herself on a path now. A path to a crucial decision. Wreak vengeance. Or not. Did she feel it strongly enough? The righteousness? The old passionate rage? It would have to possess her completely if she was going to do all that she was capable of.

Blank command field, except for the cursor. The starting point for whatever needed to happen next. Zen sat and gazed at that blinking vertical line. What demanded to be done?

No immediate answer. That was fine. There were a few things she could do while fate was brewing. Before getting started, she fetched a bandana out of a drawer and tied it over her head, covering her denuded brows.

Back to Cyberlandium. A first task had come to her: the IP address she had memorized from Mr. Walker's sticky note. It had felt so good to accuse Robert, to put all her stormy feels into that one act of blame, but with a little distance she realized how ridiculous that had been. Robert wasn't a hacker. He was an adequate gamer, and he knew more than the average middle-schooler about operating systems and such, but that was it.

On the other hand, though, why not be thorough? It would be easy to check. She knew the dates and times of her two encounters with Robert in Lukematon. If the IP address was his, it would match the logs of those sessions. Time to go back into the tunnels.

In another minute she moved once again through the old familiar grungy low-res graphic environment, abandoned as always. At the control hub she took down the dusty log-ledger for the first date and began leafing through the pages, scanning for the incriminating numbers. And, boom, just like that, there they were.

Zen jolted back into meatspace with a gasp. What? Robert was the hacker after all? But wait, no. She checked the details of the entry. The person with the address had played a couple of hours later than her first encounter with Robert, and in a different world.

So, the hacker was definitely not clueless Robert. But the hacker played on the Lukematon platform. And if vo had played before, vo was likely to play again.

Zen smiled grimly. Here was a task worthy of her skills.

Over the next several hours, Zenobia crafted a sweet little piece of code to run in the background of all the Lukematon environments, continuously scanning IP addresses. There was a simple alarm function, so she would know as soon as the hacker showed. Just for fun, she tied the scan into the presence of NPC. She test-ran it in a mothballed world, discovered one bug (a simple typo), fixed and tested again, found an infinite loop, recoded to eliminate it, and then got a clean test.

At some point the Aunties came home, first Phil, then Lucy. She deflected them both easily. Why had she come home early? Kids teasing, like she had already said. Also, feeling sick again. Better now, though, and doing homework. Writing a paper. Later they brought her dinner, granting permission to eat in her room. Aunt Phil complimented the bandana. Even later they went to bed, calling good-nights through the door.

As the hours passed, Zen felt more and more awake. It had been too long since she had enjoyed the pure, clean focus that only deep immersion in Cyberlandium brought. She grinned as she loaded her code into the Lukematon mainline. She hovered her finger over the Enter key. Always fun to have that moment of suspense. The drumroll pause. Her grin widened. As soon as she pressed the button, every bird, animal, insect, talking tree, and sentient lollipop creature (just to name a few) in a hundred worlds would be working as her spy, on eternal vigilant watch for one certain IP address entering the game environment. And, the next time the Monarch Middle School hacker came to play, she would get an alert.

She pressed Enter, wondering if the alarm would chime immediately. It did not. So, the hacker was not active this moment in Lukematon. But whenever vo showed up, she would know. Zen laughed softly, wiggling with joy at the thought of all her virtual spies doing her bidding. It felt so very good to be back in her cyber-element.

FORTY-FIVE

ONCE HER SPIES had been set to work, Zen got out of her chair and did some stretches. Sleep? No, not even close. Vengeance decision time closer now. But first, a snack.

She slipped out of her room and eased the fridge door open, reaching in to pin down the switch so that the light stayed off. In the faint city-light from the windows she browsed over the jars and boxes and bottles within, passing over the various health food options. Ha! Leftover lo mein. That would do just fine. She extracted the cardboard carton. Also a fork from an eased-open drawer, and a square of paper towel popped meticulously, one perforation at a time, from the roll.

Back in her room, munching noodles, Zen opened her mind again toward the question of what her next move might be. Hmmm. You know what? First, tunes. Who was playing what on WYZA right now? She put her headphones on and engaged the stream.

Club music. A hard-driving, snare-drum-thwacking dance

groove. As she listened, her body starting to bop, the DJ segued seamlessly into something just a little faster. Yes. This.

The next step toward the decision moment was to gather intel. Which was tied up with deciding who the targets would be.

Well, how about Natalie Davenport? She would do for a start. And that was an unusual enough last name to be useful. Who was she related to? What did they do online? What havoc could be wreaked there? Nothing truly devastating, of course. Something worthy of her reputation. Something . . . creative.

Here was someone local who might be Natalie's mom. And she ran a company. A company with a website. What the heck was a consulting firm, anyway? Didn't matter. First things first: confirm ID. School records would do for that.

Tinker tinker. Knock knock. Nope, not that way. How about . . . Yes, she was in. And indeed, Sabrina Davenport was listed as one of Natalie's parents. Surely there could only be one person with that name working in Portland. An extra moment to harvest the names of Robert's parents too, since she was in the database anyway, and then back to the Davenport website. Any chinks in the armor?

This proved a harder answer to find. Dancing a little in her chair to the overnight DJ's seemingly endless mix, she worked on it for the good part of an hour.

Then, just as she had found a way in, an annoyance, prickling at the edge of perception. Something was off about the music. What was that sound? Like a lonely sparrow trapped in the dance club, chirping in the rafters.

Wait. Bird chirping. It was her alarm. Her secret agents had spotted the hacker.

Zen bent closer over her keyboard, a mirthless grin on her face. "Got you now," she whispered. "Got you now."

No whimsical dallying this time. She used preprogrammed jumps to rocket down the tunnels. In seconds she was back in the control room. She scanned the ledger of players currently in game for the hacker's IP address. There it was. Another one of the D&D-type worlds. The hacker's character was currently located outside the entrance to the mines. There was a little country fair setup there, Zen recalled. That made this even easier. She worked a lever, turned a dial (these steampunk controls—whoever made them had a bizarre sense of humor), and then she was looking out at her suspect through the eyes of . . . checking . . . the hobbit lass behind the counter of the balloon toss. One of the throwaway games. Nothing to win. Just a way to waste some minutes, if you were that bored.

And there, presumably, was the person she was looking for. A tall, thin warrior figure, helmet down. Elf. What character name was the person playing? She hovered her cursor. Chimakedu. Hm. That was odd. And familiar. Where had she seen something like it before?

Suddenly Zen's eyes went wide. Chimakedu. Chima Kedu. Chima Kedum, that was, with the final m left off. Nine letters, stopping just short of the first repeat. And there was only one person in the whole world she could imagine choosing that name for a character.

Flabbergasted, Zen sat back in her chair and, with deliberate care, took her hand away from the touchpad. Important, right now, to think before acting. This she had not anticipated. Arli? Arli was the hacker? Could it be true?

And, if it was true, how did she feel about it? Because, yeah, hacks were illegal and memes were mean . . . but Zen also knew the pleasure of having the power to go where one was excluded and doing there what one wished. What was it Arli had said, down in the Fieldwork Sanctum? Something about revenge? Yep. And "things I'm not proud of"? Zen got up and moved agitatedly around the room. If it was Arli, what a twisty move to pick transphobic memes! A thread of self-hatred there, finding expression? Or a particularly nose-thumbing flourish, throwing everyone off the scent? Or even both at the same time?

But was it Arli? Well, it was easy to make sure. She sat down again and brought up her NPC's first line of dialog. A hawker's call—Heya, heya, step right up, try your luck. She triggered it.

The elf warrior paid no attention.

Zen clicked through her admin options. How did one write fresh lines of dialog? That? Yes. That. She clicked. A box popped up, cursor blinking in an empty field. Whatever she typed, the hobbit lass would say. She held her hands over the keyboard, considering subtleties, then decided on the direct approach. "Arli," she typed, "is that you?" She held her breath and pressed Enter.

In the wee hours of the morning, an elf warrior and a carny hobbit in a pixelated balloon-toss stared at each other. Bird-spies sang in the branches of the trees. A voice bubble appeared over the elf warrior's head. The person running the elf was typing. Words appeared. "How do you know my name?"

Zen pulled back again and gaped at her computer. A new idea began to thread through the wrangle in her mind, a thought she couldn't squelch: Hey, you know, we're already getting to be good friends. How cool would it be if we started hacking together? Went dark together? An outlaw partnership?

She still didn't quite believe it, though, and before she made her next move she wanted to make absolutely sure. She opened a chat.

Hey.

Hey. What are you doing up so late?

What are YOU doing up so late?

Couldn't sleep.
I get insomnia sometimes.
So I stay up and play games.

What kind of games?

Stuff on Lukematon, mostly.
Weird thing just happened, though.

I was playing, and I was at this little carnival place, I mean my character was, of course, and one of the carnival worker NPCs called me by name.

How could that happen?

Hello? Are you there?

Does anyone else ever use your computer?

What does that have to do with anything?

Could you please just answer the question.

No. No one else ever uses this computer.
It's mine, in my room.

Hello?

OK, I have to say it.

And then whatever happens happens.

I know what you did.

What I did?

Yes.

I'm not sure what you're talking about?

The hacks.
On the school website.

I know it was you.

Hello?

Seriously? You're accusing me of that?

After the first hack
I set up a tracker
for Mr. Walker

and the IP address is your address.
I know because that was me
talking to your elf warrior just now.

That was you?
You were spying on me?

239

I was checking. I needed to make sure.

You really think it was me.
Wow.

Are you saying it wasn't?

Doesn't matter, does it?
Because you say it is so.
You are able to think that about me.
Wow. I thought I knew you.

Don't tell me you're offended.

Um
That's not the word I would use
The word I would use
is
betrayed

Arli?

Hello?

Hello?

FORTY-SIX

WHEN ZEN OPENED her eyes, nearly tipping out of the chair, the muted gray of early morning glimmered outside the window. It had been like this before. As she slipped deeper into the Cyberlandium trance, everything else went distant, and the energy of pure focus flowed smoothly in her body and her mind. She had gone for up to three days at a time with almost no sleep, taking quick naps, then driving onward. She guessed she had been asleep for an hour, maybe two. Her neck hurt from her head hanging forward, but she felt rested.

She was hungry, though. And she needed hot water too. She was sick of smelling herself. Would the Aunties hear? No matter. It was morning. Realm of normal. The question was, did she have the emotional resources right now to face the mirror? To see her face? Let alone her body? Quick easy answer—NOPE. Not even one glimpse, thank you very much. She sighed. Time once again to practice a skill long since refined: the no-see no-feel protocol.

In the bathroom she left the light off, and as she undressed in the dim she took care to keep her eyes pointed exclusively at porous, opaque things. The towels hanging on the rack. The shower curtain with its printed design of rabbits dressed in kimonos. Once naked she also had to keep her eyes up and away from what was down there. A soap-scummed round mirror hung on a loop of plastic rope in the shower. She reached in first and turned it to the wall.

Once in, the delicious hot water sluicing down over her, she let her eyes linger on the rack of bottles, playing games with their letters to keep her eyes from straying. For example, the bottle that said "shampoo": the font they chose, if you flipped the word upside down, it looked like "oodways"—"goodways" minus the g. Arli would get a kick out of . . . Oh, wait. If they were still friends. Was Arli the hacker or not? And if vo was, why did vo react that way? Betrayed? Seriously? Wasn't that a bit extreme? What did vo think, that Zen had no sense of right and wrong at all? Come to think of it, she was feeling offended herself—feeling harshly judged by veir over-the-top reaction.

Zen frowned, pushed the thoughts away, got back to the protocol. The no-touch places were her eyebrows and one other. She let soapy water stream down through instead. And as she toweled off after, she bunched the whole towel into a bulky wad, thick enough so that she couldn't feel shapes through it. One small gift: the steam helped with the mirror situation. She wrapped one towel around her head and another around her body, snugging it tight under her arms, then eased out the door.

On her way back through the kitchen, Zen paused to extract a couple of energy bars from a cabinet she knew opened noiselessly. Her bare feet made no sound on the linoleum. Nonetheless, when she turned back, Aunt Lucy was standing in the archway from her bedroom.

Zen startled. Her hand jumped up to her forehead—yes, the towel was low enough. She wouldn't have to explain the missing brows. In her mind she groped for words to deflect and separate as quickly as possible. She so didn't want to talk to anyone right now. She had a trance going.

Except, how could she not respond to the smile her aunt was giving her? A gentle smile, with soft eyes. "Good morning, Zenobia," Aunt Lucy said, keeping her voice low for Aunt Phil, still in bed.

"Um . . . good morning."

"Are you feeling better?"

"Yes, a little. Thanks."

"Did you sleep well?"

Hardly at all, but it wouldn't do to go into that. "Yes, thank you." A pause. Manners kicked in. "How about you?"

"Middling," Aunt Lucy said. "Just middling." She sighed, pulled her robe tighter around herself, crossed to the fridge, and took out a carton of orange juice. "Oh, my mouth is dry," she said. "Would you like a glass?"

"No, thank you." Aunt Lucy poured her juice and leaned against the counter to sip it. Then she cleared her throat and said, "Zenobia, there's a question I've been meaning to ask you."

Something in the way she spoke put Zen on guard. Was this going to be something about the girl project, some pulling back? Something, even, about how Zen's living with them in their apartment might someday come to an end? The tentative, unexpected tenderness she had started to feel instantly snuffed out. Shields up. She stepped back toward her bedroom door, preparing to flee. "What?" she said.

Aunt Lucy took another moment before speaking, and Zen trembled through an adrenaline surge. Then Aunt Lucy said, "I was wondering if . . . Your Aunt Phil and I, every year we throw a Halloween party, and what I was wondering was, would you maybe like to invite some of your little friends?"

This was so different from what Zen had been dreading, it took her a couple of seconds to respond. What? A Halloween party? *Little friends?* "I am not five years old," she said coldly.

Aunt Lucy blinked. "No, I know that," she said.

Zen took another step backward. "So I'd appreciate it if you'd not treat me that way."

Aunt Lucy's brow furrowed. She opened her mouth, then hesitated. Her face closed up, and she said, "I apologize. I won't bring the idea up again."

"Good," said Zen, and turned and left the kitchen.

Safely back in her room, door locked once more, she

changed into sweats and a cotton top—the one with the huge flower. Thanks to the awkward encounter with Aunt Lucy, her quicksilver mood had returned to rageful simmer. Which suited her fine. She had more work to do.

Starting on one of the energy bars, she returned to her preparations. She had Natalie's mother's website at her mercy now. But that was only one. What about Robert? More in-game retribution? No, not enough. Something sharper was definitely called for.

With the parents' names in hand from her earlier dip into the school records, it was a short search. Crabby, bullying Mr. Grant worked at a law firm. And, my goodness—a sign-in for the admin portal, right there on the front page. It might take a while to get in, but she knew her skill. Soon she would have access to the inner workings of his company's computer network too.

FORTY-SEVEN

AUNTIE-KNOCKING WOKE her. She struggled through a moment of deep confusion. Where was she? On her bed. What, why? Oh yeah. Apparently her stamina was less than it used to be, and she had succumbed to exhaustion shortly after finding her way into Mr. Grant's computer system, sometime after a quick-grabbed lunch. She rolled and looked at the window. Evening light out there. She had slept the afternoon away.

Her mouth tasted like dirty-bathroom smell. She worked it, trying to unglue the parts, get some cleaner spit going. Another knock. "Come in," she croaked. She sounded sick. She felt sick.

The Aunties entered. Concern stated. Forehead felt. Surprise expressed at missing eyebrows—a sudden icky squirm moment. The bandana had come off while she slept. But then Aunt Phil, always so radically accepting, said, "Groovy," and went to fetch a damp washcloth. That was good. Zen's face felt cooler and cleaner after. Temp taken. Normal. Soup offered and accepted. A dinner setup appeared on the desk, laptop shoved to the side. Of course Zen had closed the screen.

After dinner she was instructed to get some more rest and call for help if she needed it. No more mention was made of silly Halloween parties, thank God. The Aunties stepped out. Zen listened to their voices on the other side of the door, discussing her. By their tones—words too faint to catch—Aunt Lucy was worried and Aunt Phil was saying it would be all right. They went away, and she was alone once more.

Revived by soup and pampering, she opened her computer screen once again. No messages from Arli. Not that she had expected any. And it didn't matter. Apparently vo wasn't the hacker outlaw she had briefly imagined ven to be, and was now off somewhere feeling all fragile and virtuous and affronted. Something about that thought made Zen feel uncomfortable—a dim sense that she was being unfair—so she pushed it away. Back to solo. Fine.

She re-accessed her work spaces and began to construct an exploit for Robert's dad's firm. No radio in headphones this time. Pure silence. Diamond clarity. Detachment. Focus. It was, in fact, like a drug. Everything else went away, and that was so exactly what she needed right now.

Three or four hours later she sat back again and stared at the eternal blinking cursor, taking a little time to reorient to reality. She massaged her hands and worked the kinks out of her shoulders and back. She needed to pee, and slipped out to accomplish this without rousing any Auntie-attention. Quiet and dark behind the curtain in the arch to their room.

Then back, and the deliberate careful typing of the single command that would set both exploits into motion. She did the Enter key finger float. She put her hand back in her lap. As always, the reverent pause. And something to do with the pleasure of power, too. *I have made a thing. I can make it go anytime I want. But I choose not to, not just yet. But I have made a thing. I can make it go.* . . . A simple looping chant. A last breath before the plunge.

Out of habit only, momentarily lulled, she picked up her phone, glanced at the screen, and read what was there before she could stop herself. A text from Arli. Time-stamped about an hour ago. Short—just two letters: FS.

Zen looked at the two letters for a long time. She looked back at the computer screen. The cursor blinked at the end of its line of characters.

She looked back at the phone. "You make me crazy," she snarl-whispered at it, at the text's sender through it. "I don't understand you. Every time I think I have you figured out, you do something else that I don't know what it means. Or how to react to it." No answer, of course. But an image rose in her mind of Arli sitting in a beanbag chair in secret candlelight. Vivid imaginary Arli looked up, tipped veir head, and did an eyebrow-quirk that said the same as words, Yeah? So, what are you going to do about it?

Zen blew out an exasperated breath. Glowered at the letters. Drummed agitated fingers on the desk.

FS.

Fieldwork Sanctum.

For Short.

Friend . . . Salvation. Zen rolled her eyes, but then resumed glowering and drumming. *Salvation.* A word with weight in her life. A word that had been used with great Meaning by others around her. She remembered a laying on of hands. She remembered a submersion. And it was true that she had felt . . . something. But, looking back now, she could not feel sure that anything had really happened. Somehow the words had just stayed words. Maybe because she had not been who they thought she was. They had saved the wrong person. A boy who didn't actually exist.

Which meant, Zen, her real self, was still free. Unsaved, but free. Free to choose her next move. It was a choice that felt like more than just what to do in the moment. It felt like the choice of who she was going to be from now on.

Press Enter, and that was a step down one path. As long as she kept to this path, she would walk alone, but she would feel safe. For whatever reason, she had been blessed with a mind that, in Cyberlandium, could wield great power. She could rule. And in Cyberlandium, the eternally excruciating puzzle of having a body that didn't match her brain just went away. It simply didn't matter.

Or, FS.

On this path, no certainty. Messy messy humans and all the confusion and risk that came with engaging with them, trying to listen to and understand them and then to say something in return. On this path, anyone, even the friend you had started to feel you could actually trust, could say the stupidest thing and whack you out into the cold. And then something you said without the least intention of causing hurt would whack that same friend out into the cold too. And then you felt . . . yes, facing it now . . . then you felt guilty and horrible and didn't know how to make it right.

What it came down to: turn away, or turn toward.

Another minute balanced on the knife edge. Zen sat and breathed. She wondered what was going to happen next. She had no idea, none at all. She only waited to see what she would do.

A little time later, the curtain blew in and out, in and out, pushed by a chilly autumn breeze in an empty room.

FORTY-EIGHT

IT HAD BEGUN to mist. Cold dampness just wet enough to take the form of tiny droplets. The streets were still busy, though. It was not too late on a Saturday night. From the bridge over the highway Zen saw many lights flowing in both directions—bright haloed headlights going one way, hazy glowing red taillights the other. She put her hoodie up over her bandana and let her walk slip back into an older stride, more hunched, the legs pistoning forward rather than swinging through the hips. Sometimes it was still useful to have a boy body. If, for example, it would be safer for someone glancing to mistake you for a boy.

As soon as she could she got off the arterial, shifting over to the quieter suburban street that paralleled it. There were some train tracks to cross. Beyond them, a sense that the elementary school was somewhere over in this direction. She wasn't sure exactly where, but as she hesitated at each corner, one choice always felt best. She knew she would find it. Meanwhile, the chilly, damp dark and the monotonous rhythm of walking blunted her mind. A wild snarl of feels lurked down inside somewhere, ready at the first provocation to surge up, but for now she let the walking and the dark soothe her riled self.

There it was. She recognized the low cinder-block buildings and the sparse grove of tetherball poles. At the front entrance bright lights shone, but around the sides and back, long stretches lay in near-darkness. That was good for a pause. Creepy shadows.

But what were the chances, really, that anyone—anyone but Arli, anyway—would be hanging out at an elementary school on a cold, wet Saturday night? She knew from life in Arizona: the dark wasn't actually all that scary. At some point she had pushed through the childhood fear, and had found the dark to be uniformly empty and quiet. Even peaceful. She moved forward again, walking as soundlessly as she could. The wet helped. Not even the tiny dry scraping of grass-blades against her sneakers.

Behind the school, yellow-tinged gray rather than black: the light of the surrounding city filtering down, reflected by the low clouds. The concrete stairwell, when she reached it, did contain at last, near the bottom, something approaching real darkness. She couldn't tell from the top if the door was open. She took a couple of breaths to work up her nerve, then descended. At the bottom she pressed gently on the door. It creaked back. Inside, absolute darkness at last.

Never without her phone, of course. As easily leave a hand behind. She activated the flashlight. That was good for some horror-movie lighting effects. The restless stark beams. The black shadows leaping and bobbling with every move. But she had spent so much of her life in tunnels of one sort or another. It felt almost homey.

She made her way through the maze, retracing the first long passage, then the twists and turns after. At length she saw the soft orange glow of candlelight ahead. One more stop to gather her strength. Then she moved forward again. She stuck her head around the last corner.

Candles flickered. Nine of them, Zen saw, counting. Arli sat in the beanbag chair opposite the one vo had had before, facing the entrance.

"Turn off your phone," vo said.

FORTY-NINE

"JEEZUM, YOU'RE BOSSY."

"Please?"

Zen turned off the flashlight.

"I mean, all the way."

"Jeezum . . ."

"Please? Seriously. It's not really away if you can still look things up and stuff."

Zen stood still a moment, then, slowly, powered her phone down. She stuck it in the pocket of her hoodie, which she then took off, being careful not to dislodge the bandana. Lastly, she wrapped the sweatshirt around the phone for extra padding. She flumped into the other beanbag chair. The same spurt of foam beads poofed up. The air was warm and stuffy and smelled of mildew and burning candles. Off down the tunnel, something ticked monotonously.

Zen looked at Arli. Away again. At again. Sometimes vo was looking back, sometimes not.

Being together without speaking felt odd, but okay. And now that she was actually looking at ven, it seemed obvious what to do. This was her friend Arli who was looking at her, with a face that had pain and anger in it, but that was also, still, open. So what if vo had lectured her so cluelessly about gender that one time? So what if vo hadn't turned out to be the hacker-companion she had briefly imagined ven to be? She had hurt her friend. She had to make it right.

Zen opened her mouth. Closed it again. Opened it again. Said, "I get it now, that you would never do such a thing. And, I'm sorry. I'm sorry that I suggested that you could."

Arli said, "You believe me. That it wasn't me."

"Yes. I believe you."

Arli's mouth trembled. "Thank you. Because, you know, I would never. Just, not."

"Okay."

"You know how I feel about the gender stuff. And Dyna is my friend. And anyway, you know I know what it's like."

"What what's like?"

"Being someone other people see as a freak. Or a threat."

More silence. Then Zen said, "Me too."

Arli met and held her eyes, but didn't speak. Vo nodded. Zen nodded back. They were taking each other's word for things, then, tonight. That felt good.

After another long silence, Arli said, "Can I tell you something?"

"Okay."

"It's . . . private. Not a thing many people know about me."

"Okay."

"And I'd appreciate if you don't mention it to anyone else."

"I won't."

They sat in silence a while longer. Then, not looking at her, Arli said, "You may have noticed I miss a lot of days of school." Vo glanced up, so Zen nodded. "Well, there's a reason. I have a thing with anxiety." Another glance, checking Zen's reaction to the word. She kept her face calm. "Not just, like, oh no, maybe something bad might happen anxiety, but really bad, crippling anxiety. Sometimes panic attacks."

One of the candles had a bouncy-flame flicker going, making the walls pulse. Arli seemed to want a response, so Zen said, "Okay? I mean, thanks for telling me. For trusting me enough to tell me. But I guess I don't have much to say."

Arli nodded.

"Except, I guess, I'm sad you have to deal with that. Because you're my friend."

Arli nodded again, and then turned away and swiped at an eye-corner. Could that tough, edgy face crumple into tears? Zen couldn't picture it. When vo faced her again, eyes dry, mouth firm. But still, the swipe.

"I mention it," Arli went on, "because I just wanted to tell you. Because, yeah, you are my friend, too." Zen nodded. "But I also mention it," Arli went on, "because I thought of something."

"What?"

"Sometimes for the panic attacks I take a pill. A serious pill, from a doctor. And it knocks me right out. I sleep without dreams and feel like I just blinked for a second and then it's morning."

"Okay."

"So what I thought was, well . . . my brother, Lynx, you remember him? If there's anyone I know who would actually do a thing like those website memes, it would be him." Zen's eyes went sharp. "I mean, he spends all this time on these message boards, and sometimes he leaves his door open when he goes to the bathroom or whatever, and I've seen images on his screen. Really gross stuff. Not just about Arab people or Muslims or whatever. Stuff about Jewish people and black and gay, too."

Zen said, "So you think maybe he's coming into your room when you're knocked out, and using your computer to hack?"

"Maybe? It's a laptop. He wouldn't even have to stay. He could take it and bring it back later."

"Hmm," Zen said. "For that to be what happened, he'd have to know when you took your pills. Would he know that?"

Arli's face had brightened some with the pleasure of speaking veir theory. Now it clouded again. "Well . . . to be honest, not usually, no."

Zen's face had gone intense. For the first time, she was really thinking about the possibility of someone besides Arli being the hacker. "There are other ways, though," she said. "Tricks and tools. Maybe we should go and have a look at your machine."

Looking at each other in the candle-wavery air, they both began to smile. Arli said, "You know, you're like a cyber-detective. You're like a young Sherlock Holmes of the Internet."

Zen blushed.

Arli said, "Can I be your Watson?"

"My what?"

"Haven't you read Sherlock Holmes? Doctor Watson. The chima detective's faithful companion and helper. I totally want to be your Watson."

Zen flapped her mouth for a moment and then managed to say, "Okay, sure. I would be honored."

"Good."

They both looked away. Zen fiddled with her hoodie strings. Her face felt hot. Something moving now inside her, some big shift. Here was a real friend. Someone she trusted. And carrying such a secret was so hard. Not just hard. Lonely. So lonely. It felt like maybe she was about to speak. Was she? She couldn't tell. She drew a breath. Yes, it seemed she was.

"I have something I'd like to tell you too."

FIFTY

CONCENTRATING ON THE two little soft knots between her fingers, rolling and squeezing them, Zen said, "Remember that time when you told me I needed to learn more about . . ." She stopped. "And just now, when I said I know, too . . ." This wasn't coming out right. She glanced up.

Patient listening face. Open and kind.

Zen looked down again and said, "I'm going to start over. Because none of that stuff matters. And actually, it's pretty simple. It's very simple, when you come right out and say it. Which I'm totally avoiding doing. But, it's time. So." One last breathing pause. Then, a straight look, eye to eye, holding the gaze, and: "I'm trans."

Arli blinked.

"My old life . . . it was bad before. But when my dad died, I got to move here, and the Aunties helped me, and I finally get to be who I am."

Arli continued to stare back, unspeaking. Zen watched

veir expression flicker. Wrinkled brow. Eyes widening, then looking up and away, maybe going along with brain remembering stuff. The start of nodding. Then, startling, a burst of goofy smile-laugh. And then suddenly Arli launched up out of veir beanbag chair and across the space between them, threw veir arms around Zen's neck, squeezed, and said, "Omigod, I must have sounded so stupid to you when I . . . but, like you said, that doesn't matter now. And I'm just so incredibly glad!"

Zen returned the hug uncertainly, patting with a hand, and surprised herself by sob-laughing. Her body, she realized, was shaking. She had been braced for . . . what? Rejection? Anger? Attack? Suddenly dropping dead because she had dared to tell her secret at last? It had felt that strong. Really. Arli rocked her back and forth a couple of times, then pulled away again. Veir face was red, veir eyes moist. They both laughed again.

Arli returned to veir beanbag, taking time to settle, getting composure back. When vo looked up again, veir face was calmer. "Thank you," vo said.

"You're welcome. Um, for what?"

"For telling me. For trusting me. Too."

"You're welcome."

"And, I'm sorry. That time when I said I was going to send you 101 stuff. That must have seemed so . . ."

"It's okay. Really. I get why you did."

Breathing slowed. Candles flickered. The air was getting uncomfortably warm. Were nine candles enough to overheat a room? Felt like.

Arli put veir face down and said, "Um, I want to say something, but I don't want you to take it the wrong way."

"Okay?"

"Because I'm not . . . I don't care . . . I'm not a romantic or dating or whatever sort of person. At all, really, I don't think. But."

"But . . . what?"

"Well, I just wanted to say, I love you."

Zen blushed and dropped her eyes.

"You are such a wonderful, amazing human, and I just really like being your friend. So, maybe better is, I friendlove you."

Zen made herself look up. "Thank you," she said. "I friendlove you too." They grinned at each other, awkward but so warm. Zen said, "If you spell it L-U-V, there're no repeats."

Arli laughed with pure delight. "Friendluv! Yes! It's perfect! I friendluv you!"

"Me too."

How to get back to regular life and talk, after such feels? Arli found a way. "You know what? I really need to pee. Let's go back to my house and do some detecting."

"Okay, let's go."

FIFTY-ONE

IT WAS CLOSE to midnight by the time they got back to the Kedum house. In the backyard, Arli whispered, "My dad's away on business, so my brother is the only one here."

"Okay," Zen said.

"And he generally stays up most of the night gaming, which the music confirms is what's happening." The manic thumping of heavy metal drums was not as loud as during Zen's first visit, but still plainly audible.

"Okay."

"Follow me."

The living room was a bleak cave of gray-yellow murk. Arli led the way through to veir room, which turned out to be small and messy. It included an unmade bed, books and fan-art drawings scattered all over, various action figures, some ornately printed cloths thumbtacked to the ceiling, and, on what looked to be a desk left over from little-kid days, a laptop computer.

Before getting down to sleuthing they took turns slipping across the hall into the bathroom. During her crossing, Zen peered through the gloom down to Lynx's door at the end of the hall. It was festooned with stickers mostly in black and silver. The drums banged relentlessly behind it. Nothing to see or guess from that closed portal.

In the room again, Zen asked with a touch of formality, "May I examine your computer?"

Arli looked puzzled. "Of course. That's why we're here."

"I mean, dig into files and stuff. Anything private in there?"

"Oh. I see what you mean. No, it's okay. Nothing I'd be embarrassed to have you see, except some bad fan fic."

"We won't need to go there," Zen said, sitting down.

She had a routine with new machines: check out hardware and operating system, review running background processes and executable files in a few key lists and folders. It all looked completely normal on first scan, if out-of-date. "You're going to need a new computer soon," she said, her voice rather robotic. Already sinking into the Cyberlandium-spell. "If you want to keep playing all your favorite games."

"I so wish," said Arli. "Not likely, though, anytime soon."

Zen had already moved on. First stop: Arli's browser of choice. This might be super-simple. A quick check of browsing history could do it. But, no—the oldest entry was only a few days old. Zen said, "Do you ever clear your history?"

Arli said, "No. I don't know how. Should I?"

"Maybe? From time to time? But that's not the point. Your history has been cleared, so someone else has been using your machine."

"So, like I said? My brother, sneaking in?"

"No, not necessarily. Doesn't have to be him. And doesn't mean whoever it was actually used the computer in person. Could be a RAT."

"A rat?"

"R-A-T—remote access trojan. A program to control one machine from another one."

"As in, I smell a rat? Or, you dirty rat?" Zen, jostled out of her trance, gave her friend an annoyed look. Vo was grinning a hard grin. "Should we put out some rat traps? Call the ratcatcher?"

"Could you please stop?"

"Well, excuse me."

Already reentering trance, Zen said sternly, "I need you to be quiet now. I have to work." Arli, abashed, subsided. Zen turned back to the machine and began a systematic deep search.

The minutes ticked by. The loudest sounds were the thudding of Lynx's music and the clicking of keys and mouse. Arli fidgeted but stayed quiet. Then Zen said, "Ha. Got you now."

"What?"

"What I thought. Remote access program. One of the more clever ones. Hard to find." A note of pride in her voice.

"So, is it Lynx? Because, now that I think about it, if it is him, he's framing me. That is so not cool."

"The only way I can tell is by going the other way through the pipe and seeing where it leads."

"And if it is him, would he know we were looking?"

"Probably not? I should be able to check without him noticing."

"But he might."

"Yeah, he might."

Zen waited. Arli began beating a hand on a knee, frown deepening. At last vo said, "Do it. I need to know."

More minutes of intent typing and clicking. Arli plucked a random rubber band from a bedside crate, lay back on the bed, and started softly shooting it toward the ceiling and catching it again.

At length Zen said, "I'm in."

"And?"

"Well, what I can do now is, I can bring what's on the other screen up on our screen. Maybe we could tell from that."

Arli swung around so vo could see. "Do it."

Zen clicked. The screen switched. Whoever it was was playing a game. It appeared to be set in a prison. "I know this game," Zen said. "It's on Lukematon."

"What is it?"

"Prison planet game. You can play a prisoner plotting to escape with other prisoners, or you can play one of the guards. It's really violent and bloody. Yuck."

Arli had frozen. In a tight voice vo said, "It's him."

"It is? How can you tell?"

"Username. That's his username." Vo pointed. Under the side picture of a particularly hulking bruiser of an avatar, all distorted veiny muscles, it said, "EliteStormTrooper666."

"Really?" said Zen.

"Really."

"Jeezum."

FIFTY-TWO

ZEN SAT BACK away from the machine. She tipped her head and quirked her mouth: So, what do you want to do about it?

Arli scrunched veir face and shook veir head: I don't know.

"Turn him in?" Zen said out loud.

"Ehhh . . ." Arli said. "Not the best choice for me. It's already seriously no fun in this house most of the time, what with my gender thing, and just general sibling stuff. Unless they'd, like, throw him in jail for five or six years, until I was old enough to leave home?"

"I don't think that's going to happen."

"Yeah, me neither."

They pondered together. Zen asked, "Would talking to him directly be a good idea?"

"No." Flat and final.

"Okay," Zen said. She turned back to the computer and stared at it. She said, "What if he turned himself in?"

"Right," Arli said. "Like that's ever going to happen."

"No, I can probably arrange it." Not bragging. Just saying.

"You can?"

"Yes. You're not the only one with a key to secret tunnels."

Arli looked puzzled and unconvinced. Zen said, "Wanna see?"

"Okay."

Zen returned the display to their own computer. Click. Click click. Password one. Password two. Secret key. They were in. Second set of low murky mysterious passages of the evening. Arli scooched a little closer. "So cool . . ." vo breathed.

Zen typed a few more commands, and they found themselves in the virtual prison cell, this time as invisible admins, watching the guard played by Arli's brother as he beat a prisoner. Zen did the finger-interlace-reverse-hand knuckle crack, looked at Arli, and said, "Okay, watch."

In another moment, she had an empty dialog box open. "This guard is about to get a radio call," Zen said. "From a commanding officer. I'm just going to say"—she leaned forward and typed—"'Urgent. EliteStormTrooper666, report to the warden's office immediately.'" She pressed Enter.

On the screen, the guard's radio squawked. They watched the uniformed gorilla-man stop whaling on the prostrate body before him and put the radio to his ear. He listened. Then he let himself out of the cell and headed in the direction of the warden's office. Invisibly, Zen and Arli followed.

The warden had a secretary. Finding her rhythm now,

Zen slipped virtually inside him as Lynx entered the room. Time for face-to-face dialog.

Lynx's avatar spoke. "The warden wanted to see me."

"Yes," Zen had the secretary say. "Please have a seat."

Arli snickered. "You're gonna make him wait?"

"Yes."

They watched Lynx's guard fidget in the too-small seat. Arli said, "What else can you do?"

"Pretty much anything, within the architecture of the game."

"Like, could you, I don't know . . . turn off the lights?"

"Sure." Arli was doing expectant-face, and Zen wanted Lynx to wait a bit longer, so she brought up the controls for the room and turned off the light. She turned it back on. Lynx's guard looked up at the fixture. Zen clicked several times with the mouse and the lights flicked off-on-off-on-off-on. Lynx's guard jumped to his feet, and Arli laughed.

"Could you make something random appear in the room?"

"I could."

"Like, say, a bunny?"

Zen knew that she was showing off, but what the heck. A bunny was trickier than the lights, but in another minute a rabbit borrowed from another world popped into being on the secretary's desk. A voice balloon appeared over Lynx's guard's head: "What the hell is going on?" Zen clicked again and another bunny joined the first. She clicked several more times, until the desk overflowed with bunnies. "I love it!" Arli crowed.

Lynx's character looked plenty agitated now. Zen deleted the bunnies, then brought the dialog box back up and had the secretary say, "The warden will see you now." Into the office they all trooped.

The warden was a fearsome-looking man, muscles just as absurdly over-rendered as Lynx's, plus crew cut, scowl, and cigar. He wore a huge handgun on his hip. He stood up as Lynx came in.

"You wanted to see me, sir?"

Zen looked at Arli. "Last chance to not do this," she said.

"Do it. Oh please please, do it."

"Yes," Zen typed. "EliteStormTrooper666, or should I say, Lynx Kedum, something troubling has come to my attention." One more glance at Arli before pressing Enter. Arli nodded eagerly. Enter.

A long silence. Then, "How do you know my name?"

"I know all about you, Kedum."

"Who the hell is this?"

"I know what you did."

"Who the hell is this?? What are you talking about?"

"And even on this planet, we have standards of decency, Kedum."

Lynx was apparently stunned into wordlessness.

"Putting those memes on the school website. What were you thinking, you scum?"

The avatar just swayed and stared.

Zen began to type another line. The door banged open. Not the virtual door. The real door. Arli shrieked and jerked back on the bed. Lynx's music suddenly louder. Lynx himself standing in the doorway. He did a double take at Zen. Then he demanded, "Are you snowflakes spying on me?"

FIFTY-THREE

ZEN LUNGED TO close the Lukematon window, but it was too late. The warden's office scene was clearly visible from where Arli's brother stood. "What the hell is this?" Lynx said. "Some weird rabbit glitch, and then I see the RAT link is active, and . . . and who are you, anyway?" This last addressed to Zen. "Wait, I've seen you before. Yeah, the ride I gave, right?"

Zen glanced at Arli, who was shaking veir head slowly and doing a look that said, We are so totally screwed.

Zen was not so sure. She felt afraid of Lynx the human person, fuming there in the doorway, but in Cyberlandium she knew she owned him. The trick was, how to get this confrontation safely back to the virtual. To gain a few seconds while her mind worked, she answered the question. "Yes, that's right."

"What's your name?"

"Zenobia."

"And what are you doing here?"

"I came for a sleepover with Arli."

Arli opened veir mouth to confirm the story, but Lynx got in first. "No, I mean, what are you doing . . . here?" He pointed to the computer.

Zen and Arli exchanged another look. Arli's face said, Whatever you're thinking of, don't do it. Zen said mildly, "Would you like to see?"

"What are you, some kind of little script kiddie?"

This jab was all Zen needed to cement her decision. Time to show her strength. The fierce, hot joy rose up in her, and she tightened her mouth against the smile that wanted to bloom there. No need to humiliate. Don't overplay it. Just demonstrate skill. She turned to the computer, reopened the Lukematon screen. Arli shrank back against the wall as Lynx stepped up behind her. Zen ignored the prickle of danger at the back of her neck and said in a calm, almost chatty voice, "I have admin access to Lukematon. See?" She panned around the warden's office. Lynx's guard still stood in front of the desk. "I can do anything you can do in the game," she said. She opened the guard's satchel. "What's this? An Uzi?" she said. "You don't need this." She deleted the weapon.

"Hey!" barked Lynx. Arli squeaked. Zen felt her chair jiggle as the older boy's hand gripped it, but she kept her eyes forward. "But that's not all," she said. "I can also do things you can't do. Like the bunnies, for instance." She repopulated the office with bunnies. "Or," she said, keeping her voice carefully light—the moment of greatest danger, she sensed, was approaching, the tipping point where he would either accept her control or fight—"or, for example, I can change your avatar." She opened a new panel, scrolled through choices, and replaced his veiny muscle-locked hulk with a skinny little sickly looking dude.

Lynx uttered a string of curse words, and the chair shook again, but when Zen glanced at him, she saw he had stepped back a pace. "That's not real," he said. "There's no way a kid like you could do that." His face still had anger in it, but also, now, the first shade of doubt.

Still holding back the smile, Zen shrugged and said, "Go look."

Lynx stared at her, then, reluctantly, backed away and disappeared down the hall to his room.

As soon as he was gone, Arli hissed, "Are you crazy? He's going to kill me!"

"What choice did we have? He caught us."

"Oh, this is very, very bad."

Zen shook her head. "No, listen," she said. "He doesn't understand yet how much I can do to him. You don't either." Arli still looked appalled. "Okay, for example, he hangs out on some of the boards, right?" Arli nodded. "Because I have admin access to a couple of them, too." She turned to the computer again, opened another window, and did some rapid typing and clicking. The banner popped up for one of the more toxic gathering places of girl-gamer haters and racist meme-makers. More fierce typing. Lynx had been gone for a while.

Probably still trying to change his avatar back. "Yep," Zen said. "Here he is. EliteStormTrooper666. So, even more leverage. I can do anything to him here, too."

Arli was finally starting to get a grip on veirself. "So, if he does anything to me . . ."

"I can make his online life hell."

Down the hall, the music stopped. Zen minimized the new window. Footsteps. Lynx reentered the room. "Change it back," he growled.

"No."

Lynx made a fist and stepped forward. Arli quailed against the wall. Zen flinched, but held her ground. Time to close. She wished she and Arli had had a little more time to talk, to work out the details. But it was going to be all right. "I can erase you," she said calmly. "In Lukematon. Any game. All games." She swiveled, clicked. The new window she had just opened popped up. "But that's not all," she said. "This is you, right?"

Lynx had gone absolutely still, but his face answered the question.

"Thought so," Zen said. "Here, too, I can erase you. Or make you say or do whatever I want."

"I don't believe you!"

"Want me to show you?" Zen said. She clicked twice. A dialog popped up. "What shall I have you say?" she asked. "How about if I have you do a post to the general list, confessing that you're gay?"

"No! Don't do that!" Now, for the first time, Lynx looked afraid.

Zen, seeing the change, said, "So, here's how it's going to go." Improvising, but it felt important to follow through while he was feeling most vulnerable. "Number one: you're going to write an email to the school, admitting it was you who did the hacks, and promising never to do it again."

Lynx opened his mouth to speak, but Zen held up a finger, and he shut it again. Zen felt another pulse of pleasure. She worked to keep her voice steady. "Number two: if you ever do anything to hurt my friend Arli, I will make you pay for it." Now Lynx was shaking his head, but his face had a hunted look. Zen said, "You've only seen a little of what I can do. Think about it. There's only one way out of this."

A long, ragged-breathing silence. Lynx looked back and forth between Arli and Zen. The two friends watched him struggle. His shoulders went up, like he was thinking of fighting again, but then they slumped, and his face changed, and his head jerked down and up once. "By Monday," Zen said, still improvising. "Monday at noon." Another tight, unwilling nod.

Lynx's body language said he wanted to leave now. Before going, though, he cleared his throat and said, "Um . . . could you change me back?" He gestured at the computer. After a pause, he added, "Please?"

Zen nodded, closed the board window, and switched back to Lukematon. Click, click, click: his avatar went back to hulking bruiser. Lynx, watching over her shoulder, could not suppress a wordless sound of admiration. "And," he said tentatively, "the gun?"

Zen's answer was to take her hands away from the keyboard. The message was clear: Don't forget. Don't start thinking you can get out of this. I own you. After a second, he understood and fled.

FIFTY-FOUR

ARLI SAID, "THAT was incredible. You have such power. I am in awe."

Glowing pink, Zen said, "Thank you." But then her face clouded again, and she said, "Are you going to be all right?"

Arli's eyes shifted toward Lynx's room, back again. "I think so?" vo said. "He's all angry and closed up most of the time, but I don't think he's all that dangerous. Yet. And anyway: what you did. He can't get out of it. So, I feel safe. As safe as I ever do, anyway."

Zen yawned. She glanced at the corner of the screen. It was after one a.m. "Good," she said. "But I'm still going to text you in the morning."

"Okay." Arli yawned too. "It's a pretty long walk back to your house," vo said. "Do you want to stay?"

"I can't. The Aunties would have a conniption."

"Okay." Then good-nights and good-byes, and a sleepy passage through dark, quiet streets, the climb back through the window, and—after carefully deleting the string of characters still waiting on her command line—Zen floated down into sweet unconsciousness in her own bed, humming with the pleasure of power exercised for good.

Voices in the kitchen woke her. The endless stream of company. The guest in the kitchen turned out to be Uncle Sprink again, there to join them for Sunday brunch.

Once the meal was underway, he said to Zen, "What's with the do-rag, sugar?" She stared at him for a moment, uncomprehending. Then she remembered and blushed. "I mean, it's a look, and I do like the print of the fabric, but honestly, honey, it looks like you slept in it."

Aunt Phil said, "Chickadee, you should show your uncle Sprink. Maybe he can help."

For a second Zen felt aware only of the desire to flee. But then she made herself scan from face to face around the table. She saw three pairs of eyes without the least hint of meanness in any of them.

"I . . . Um, this is so embarrassing. . . . These kids at school, they were teasing me about my eyebrows. Someone made a gif." Aunt Lucy said a sharp word under her breath. "The caterpillar thing, it really got to me. So I came home and found the tweezers in the bathroom and started pulling out eyebrow hairs, and then, I don't know what happened, it got all weird, and I couldn't figure out how to get it exactly even, and pretty soon . . . well . . . there wasn't anything left." Uncle Sprink was nodding.

Zen made her hand go up and pull off the bandana. Eyes. All the eyes. But, still, no meanness in them. Aunt Phil was doing the wrinkle-scrunchy empathy face she did. It was Uncle Sprink, though, who broke the silence. "Girlfriend, is that all?" he said cheerfully. "Sweetheart. Not to worry. I can so help you with that."

"You can?"

"Well, sure, of course." He tipped his head. "Let me guess, I bet you'd love to have this sorted out by tomorrow morning before school, right?"

"Yes," said Zen ardently. "I would."

"All right then. I don't have my kit with me now, but how about if I come back this evening?"

The Aunties were nodding. "Okay?" Zen said. "Thank you?" She wasn't sure what was being offered. Was it makeup? Did he really know about that?

Well, only one way to find out.

And that was all about eyebrows. It took Zen a minute or two more to get her composure back, but there was an abundance of warmth in the room, and soon she was joking and laughing again.

Are you there?

Yeah, I'm here.

Everything OK?

Yes, everything's fine.

Good. I was worried.

I know. Thanks.

You're welcome.

So, I have to ask:
How does he seem today?
Your brother.

It's funny you should ask me that, because something really weird happened this morning.

?

Well, you remember, my dad's gone for the weekend, so it's just the two of us. And I was eating breakfast at around 10 a.m. and he came in, and at first I thought he wasn't even going to look at me, let alone talk to me, but then he stopped and looked at me and his face was so different.

Different how?

Like, he's so angry all the time, but now
he looked like how he used to be when we
were both a lot younger, and he said—I still
can't believe this—he said:
You are so lucky.

Say what now?

Yeah.
And I just kind of gaped at him, and then I said,
What do you mean? And he said, You're only in
middle school, and you've already figured it out.
So I said, Figured what out?

And he said, Who you are!
Vo ven veir and all that.
And I said, Wait, are you jealous of me?
And he said, I'm three years older than you,
and I have no idea.

Big eyes wow face.
So is he going to write the email?

I don't know. That was the end of the
conversation. He went back into his room,
and I haven't seen him since.

That's amazing.

Yeah.
I haven't seen him, um, act like a human
for a couple of years.

That's a sad thing to say. About anyone.

I know, right? Sad a couple ways.
Like, I didn't realize how used I've gotten to him
just sort of being gone. Like he died, almost.

You there?

Yeah, sorry, thinking about what I just typed.
And the other part is, turns out he's still alive in
there, inside the hard shell he has made, and
all I can think of is

Hello?

Long pauses

Yeah
All I can think of is
He must be so lonely.

If you say so.

But it was still awful what he did.

I'm not going to argue with you about that.

FIFTY-FIVE

BEFORE DINNER, IN the bathroom, Zen looked at her face in the mirror. Never easy or fun, but at least she could look again, now that Uncle Sprink was going to do . . . whatever he was going to do. And she had never had the chance to play with that before. So, just maybe this was going to be really good.

Dinner was quiet. The Aunties read at the table sometimes, and Zen had recently started doing the same. Another thing that had never happened in her old life, but nice. As long as you had a book that didn't want to close all the time. And she was still learning to be careful about getting sauce blips on the pages.

Then the buzzer buzzed, and Uncle Sprink was there. He had a metal case with him, like a toolbox in its rugged construction and many latches. He opened it with a flourish to reveal dozens of bottles with different-colored stuff inside, intriguingly shaped canisters, flat boxes with clear plastic lids, and ranks and rows of brushes of many different shapes. They ranged from tiny pointed ones like a watercolor painter might use for fine details up to huge bushy ones like her dimly remembered great-grandpa had used to put shaving cream on his face.

Taking charge, Uncle Sprink turned on all the lights, then placed one of the dining table chairs in the middle of the kitchen floor and sat her in it. For himself he borrowed the office chair from her bedroom so he could roll around her. Aunt Lucy had some work to do and sat in the living room with her laptop. Aunt Phil stayed in the kitchen, drawing out the finishing of the dishes, and then took a seat with a cup of tea near at hand. When Zen glanced at her, she gave back a twinkling smile of encouragement.

Once Uncle Sprink had his supplies arrayed on the table, he sat face to face with Zen and said, "Okay, eyebrows. Hold this." He handed her an oval hand-mirror. "I'll do the first one, so you can see how, and then you do the second. Work for you?"

"Yes, s— Yes, thank you."

It was strange, having his big stubbly man-face so close, but fine once she got used to it. What was stranger was that he was that close but so completely not looking at her. Or, not into her eyes, the way a person would who was talking to you. He stared instead with intense concentration at the place just above her eyes. She could hear his breath whistling minutely through his nose. He smelled nice, close up. Man smell, like her father, but with a touch of perfume, too. His eyes blinked to hers for a second, seeing her again. He smiled. "Okay?"

"Okay."

"And, you know, honey, next time, when they grow out again, you can use scissors too. Trim and pluck both, to get the shape you want."

Abashed that she hadn't come up with this simple idea herself, Zen mumbled, "Oh. Right. Okay. Thanks."

His eyes had gone above hers again. She watched in the mirror as, with a brown pencil, he sketched in an arched line over her eye. It ran along the upper edge of where the old eyebrow had been. The pencil point dug gently into her skin, with a waxy feel. It was an odd sensation, but it didn't hurt at all.

Next he began to thicken and shape the line. He made it broadest where the peak was, just inside the center line of the eye. He drew delicately. Not an outline colored in—individual hairlike lines. All of a sudden, she could see what he was doing taking shape. She gasped a little. He said, "That good? I'm flattered," and Aunt Phil, watching, chuckled.

A few more judicious dabs with the pencil, and Zen had a new left eyebrow, higher, thinner, and archier than her old one. It was pretty. She marveled at how, underneath it, her eye had so much more room to be an eye.

"Okay, your turn, sweetheart," he said, and the tutorial began.

It was harder than it looked—holding the mirror, managing the pencil, and especially figuring out how to deal with the backward-in-the-mirror thing. The pencil point kept going the opposite direction from what she wanted, until she had a collection of random marks around her target spot. It looked like a regular eyebrow that had been flattened by a teensy face tornado. She growled.

"No worries," Uncle Sprink said. "We can erase it and start over." He took a moist pad out of a screw-top jar and scrubbed with it, and the skin above her right eye was clear once more. "You know what?" he said. "You should practice doing this in the bathroom mirror. Easier, because you don't have to hold it. Also, it's where you'll do this on your own." Zen looked at him with dawning hope, and he said, "Well, of course, darling. I'll leave the pencil. That was the point, right? To go to school tomorrow looking your best."

"Yes," Zen breathed.

On the way into the bathroom, Zen wondered something she had wondered a few times before. Did he know? Had the Aunties told him? Or had he figured it out for himself? And, should she ask? Yesterday the answer still would have been an emphatic no. But yesterday she hadn't come out to Arli. Her heart beat faster. She said, "Uncle Sprink, I don't know if . . . Do you . . ." She ground to a halt.

Their eyes met in the mirror. "What's up, sweetie?" he said.

Gulp. "You . . . you do know that I'm trans, right?"

His expression remained calm. "No, I didn't know," he said. A pause. "Well, how 'bout that." And then, "Okay, let's try again, shall we?"

As she began her second effort, Zen frowned a little bit, surprised to discover herself feeling a touch of . . . disappointment? Was that the feeling? Yes, it seemed to be. Disappointment about what?

Disappointment that he hadn't been . . . impressed?

She frowned a little more. No big deal, his reaction said. Meh. Whatever. Slowly, Zen smiled. Now that she thought about it, she liked that reaction a lot.

Her second try went better. Touching her face with her other hand helped her to guide the pencil, and she did her best to draw the mirror image of what he had drawn on the other side. A couple of minutes passed in tongue-poked-out intensity. Then she pulled back and studied her handiwork. She turned her head to look from different angles. She tweaked in one small correction. In the mirror, Uncle Sprink was nodding. "Really good," he said, and grinned at her. "You've got a knack for this."

She turned and faced him. "Are you sure?" she said.

He crouched down so his face was level with hers and stared at her forehead, his eyes switching back and forth. He nodded again. "Fabulous," he said. "Spot on, darling."

Zen laughed, and then impulsively hugged him. He was solid and warm and bristly and squeezable. He put an arm around her and squeezed back. "Thank you," she said.

"No problemo, sweetheart," he said. "Let's go show the Aunties."

FIFTY-SIX

THE AUNTIES WERE warmly appreciative, and Zen soaked up the love. But then she noticed that Uncle Sprink was staring at her face again, and her joy dropped a notch. "What?" she said. "Did I smudge it?" Her finger darted to her brow.

"Ah-ah!" Uncle Sprink said, and, startled, she yanked her hand away again. "Don't touch, honey," he went on in a softer voice. "Trust your work, and don't touch." Then he added, "And, no, nothing's wrong." He tilted his head the other way, still looking. "It's just that, now that I look, you do have a really lovely face—I know some girls who would kill for those cheekbones—and your proportions are excellent. So if you'd like, just for fun, we could do a little more." He gestured back toward the kitchen again. "How 'bout it? Wanna play?"

Zen saw the eager light in his eyes and thought, Why, you're a makeup geek.

"I don't know, Sprink," Aunt Lucy said. "Your usual

style . . . wouldn't it seem a little out of place on such a young face?"

Uncle Sprink put his hands on his hips and said in mock outrage, "Honey! What do you take me for?" Then in his regular voice again he said, "No, trust me. I know exactly how to play this. An already beautiful face, with the potential for a look that's truly stunning. Not glam. Real glamour."

"Um, you know . . ." Zen said. Three pairs of eyes looked at her. She felt her cheeks go warm, but said what she was thinking. "You know, I wouldn't mind maybe trying glam one time."

Uncle Sprink smiled. "Well, sure," he said. "But there really is a difference. We take you over the line, it wouldn't do to show up at school like that. Maybe for Halloween or something, though."

Aunt Phil said, "Maybe for our Halloween party next week."

Zen looked at Aunt Lucy. "You said about that before," she said. "And I thought you meant something for little kids."

"I know that's what you thought," Aunt Lucy said. "But you seemed like you weren't in the mood to have me tell you otherwise, so I didn't press the point."

Zen blushed, remembering how cold she had been. But Aunt Lucy didn't seem angry. "So it's . . ." She waved a hand, meaning, For adults too, for everyone?

"Well, sure, cupcake," said Aunt Phil warmly. "Us Rainbow People, we take Halloween seriously."

"Absolutely!" said Uncle Sprink. "Be whoever you want to be! It's like our New Year's Day, our national holiday."

Zen looked back at Aunt Lucy. "I'm sorry I didn't get it before," she said. "Would it be too late to ask my friends?"

"Not at all," said Aunt Lucy. "Of course you can."

"Right on," said Aunt Phil.

Zen turned back to Uncle Sprink, feeling shy, but determined to speak her hope. "And could you . . . maybe . . . could we play with glam then?"

Uncle Sprink grinned at her. "Sure, of course. But in the meantime"—he gestured toward the kitchen chair again—"shall we?"

So Zen sat back down in the chair, and Uncle Sprink got to work. No mirror this time. "I want you to see it all at once," he said. Then his face went cool, distant.

First he clipped her hair back. Then, with many quick pats of a little pad, he applied powder all over her face. Next, the brushing of a darker pinkish-red powder below her eyes, as well as a few other strategic spots. Then long, detailed work around her eyes, first with a thing like a thin, inky pen-brush, and then color on pad-brushes—color with a dash of sparkle in it—and mascara applied with an applicator held in a hand gripped at the wrist by the other hand. He spoke only to give commands or reprimands. "Close your eyes." "Don't blink!" "Look up." "Look down." "Turn this way." "Hold your head straight." "Don't touch!" His voice was sharp, but Zen could hear that it wasn't mean. Just intense. He simply cared so much about what he was doing.

A pause to stare at his work so far, nudging her chin to turn her face to different angles. Some adjustments to the mascara.

Next he pulled out what looked like a skinny red pen, which he used to draw an outline around her lips. And, finally, with another soft pencilly thing, he colored them in.

Zen was squirming by now, yearning to see what he was doing. She still had to wait, though. Uncle Sprink pulled out a hairbrush, unclipped her hair, and brushed it back. He frowned at it, pulled out some hairspray, and brushed her hair the other way, with a part to the side and the length held in place with judicious spritzes from the spray can. Zen jiggled in her seat. "Hold still!" She held still.

By now both Aunties were watching intently. Aunt Phil whispered something to Aunt Lucy, who nodded and went into her bedroom. She came back with a pair of dangly ear-rings. They had silver spirals with blue beads in the centers. They looked antique. Zen loved them at once. Aunt Lucy said, "Zenobia, I forgot to tell you—these came in the mail the other day. From Grandma Gail. With a sweet note, asking if you might like them."

"Really?"

"Really. She's had them for a long time. I remember from when I was a child." Zen drew in a sharp breath, suddenly near tears. Uncle Sprink, reading her expression, gave her a look that said, Don't cry! She did her best to press the feels down again, and let her aunt put the earrings in her ears, free just this week from the little trainer-balls.

At last Uncle Sprink stepped back and stared hard at her one last time. Then, smiling, he handed her the mirror, face-down. "Okay, honey," he said gently. "Go ahead and look."

Zen was trembling. All those years of dreading the mirror. Never knowing how much boy she would see. Always, there was some. Always. On good days, only a little, so that she could put her shoulders back and go out and face the day, carrying the burden but showing up. On bad days, only able to glance for a moment, the boyness bursting out everywhere, coarse, awful, wrong, unerasable. So it had always been.

She turned over the mirror. She gasped. Her hand flew to her mouth, then down again so she could continue to gaze at what she was seeing.

Really? Was it really her? Really really really?

Looking back at her in the mirror was a girl. A girl with a face. A face that moved as her face moved, so that she had to see, had to begin to believe, that it was her.

Her hair, soft and flowing, framing the sweet inverted teardrop shape. Skin smooth and radiant. Pretty, full pink lips with a touch of smile even when she wasn't smiling. And, the eyes, framed in a delicately crafted black outline and artful color all around, huge and lustrous.

But, best of all: not even the tiniest scrap of boy-face left.

Her eyes flitted quickly to all the problem spots: brows, nose, upper lip, chin, jaw. She couldn't see boy even when she tried.

Zen's breath came faster and harsher. Her eyes were suddenly wet. "Don't cry, honey," Uncle Sprink said, but there was no stopping these tears. Aunt Phil came over, offering arms to wrap, a side to lean into. Zenobia clutched her and sobbed.

"You're beautiful, twiglet," murmured Aunt Phil. "So pretty. So gorgeous. Such a beautiful girl."

The way Aunt Phil was holding her, Zen was looking at Aunt Lucy, who gazed intently back. Through her tears, Zen mouthed, Beautiful?

Aunt Lucy smiled and did a little head waggle, with maybe some yes and no in it, but mostly just, Does it matter? Then her face became still again, almost stern, and she mouthed back, Girl.

Another sob burst up inside Zen. Yes, that was it. Beauty was something she had hardly dared to think about yet. That was running, which came after walking, which came after crawling. And it didn't matter nearly so much right now as the simple fact that what she had just seen in the mirror was girl.

Girl and nothing but girl.

All girl.

Just.

Girl.

FIFTY-SEVEN

SHE HAD TO erase the magical face. After many selfies from many angles, of course. "You can't sleep in it, honey," Uncle Sprink said. "It would look like hell in the morning, and you'd probably just have to throw away the pillowcase." So, reluctantly, she submitted to the wiping away of the sweet, deep vision of self his talent had given her. He left her supplies, though: the pencil for drawing eyebrows, complete with sharpener, some pads for erasing them again at night, and some eye shadow and lip gloss too, just for fun, with tips on how to use them correctly.

Doing the eyebrows again was the first thing she thought of when she woke. The first try she drew them too high, and had to laugh at the expression of comical surprise she had created. She scrubbed them off and tried again. There really was just one spot that was exactly right, that brought her eyes out and made them glow. On the second try she found it. She added a little eye shadow and lip gloss and looked again. Not over-the-top glamour-gorgeous like last night—just natural girl coming out more, in a subtle but real way. She smiled and reached for the hairbrush.

Walking to school, her mood continued equal parts giddy and warm. Under wraps, though. There was no way it wouldn't be awkward with Mr. Walker and especially with Robert. And Lynx was on her mind. Her invented-in-the-moment deadline of noon today had almost arrived, and she was feeling uncomfortably aware of the holes in her improvised plan. How would they know if he had written the email? What would they do if he didn't? She wanted badly to talk to Arli, but couldn't find ven before the bell.

The first thing that happened when she entered Mr. Walker's room actually turned out to be eye contact with Elijah. He gave her a shy little nod. She nodded back, and wondered what it might be like to come out to him, too. Even bubbling inside with giddy warmth, she still pulled back at the thought of that. Although, it could be good, too. To talk to someone who really understood. So yeah, someday.

Mr. Walker called class to order. "Before we get started," he said, "I have an update for you all about the website situation." Zen sat up straighter, heart suddenly beating hard. "This morning Principal Vann received an email from someone admitting to the hacking." A murmur passed through the room. Zen couldn't help glancing at Robert. He scowled back at her. Okay, it wasn't over then, with him. But that was fine. It felt clarifying, having an enemy, and in this one arena at least she knew her strength. She gave him a little nod and a touch of a smile. His face went puzzled.

Mr. Walker continued, "The email said the person was sorry and wouldn't do it again."

Zen didn't dare utter a word, but fortunately someone else asked: "Who was it?"

"The email was anonymous, but I read it, and it contained information that helped us feel sure that it was from the person." Details only the hacker would know, Zen thought. But the anonymous part, that was a bit of a problem. She had assumed Lynx would make a full confession, say who he was. But had she instructed him to do it that way? Now that she thought about it, she couldn't feel sure that she had. She felt the need to talk to Arli.

Arli clearly had the same idea, because vo was waiting outside the door when Zen came out of class. They stepped around a corner into a little-used side hall. Arli couldn't hide veir glee as vo said, "We got him! He confessed."

"Yes." They shared a look, savoring triumph. But then Zen had to speak her concern. "The only thing is, he did it anonymously."

Arli's grin faded. "Anonymously? I didn't hear that part."

"Yes."

"Oh. Hmm." A pause. "This is weird. It's like—"

"—we have to decide if it's good enough."

"Yeah. We have to judge."

"I don't like judging," Zen said. "It makes me feel squidgy."

"I don't mind it. At least not this time." Arli thought about it. "Honestly, there's a part of me that just wants him to suffer. He's a terrible brother."

"Are you talking about revenge? Because recently I've figured out that that makes me feel squidgy too."

"Not revenge. Justice."

"What's the difference?"

"Um, I guess maybe, because what he did didn't hurt us personally? That would be revenge, right?"

"But still. We are not the police. Not the court. Not the jail."

"Yeah, I get your point."

They pondered together. Then Zen said slowly, "I think it's good enough. Mr. Walker told us he said he was sorry and that he wouldn't do it again."

Arli nodded. "Okay," vo said. "I agree." The bell rang. Time to run to their next classes. All of a sudden Zen really wanted to give Arli a hug. The blocking was wrong, though, so she just did a kind of shoulder-bump thing. "We can always do something else later if we think we have to," she said.

"Okay, yeah," Arli said. "Good."

FIFTY-EIGHT

NEXT MEANINGFUL ENCOUNTER in a day destined to be full of them: coming around a corner and finding herself suddenly face to face with Natalie and a couple members of her posse.

Perhaps it was best that she had no time to prepare herself for that hostile, presumptuous stare. Given time to think, she might have second-guessed herself, talked herself into a less bold course. As it was, roller coaster so high, she followed her first natural instinct, which was to stand up straighter and stare right back.

A quick little drama played out on Natalie's face. Momentary surprise, followed by quickly surging smugness, but then a glance at Zen's eyebrows, followed by the least little double take, just a flicker of the eyes, and the draining away again of smugness. The reliable bullying-hook was gone. Zen's eyebrows no longer looked like caterpillars. In fact (as she had just confirmed on her phone for the hundredth time) they looked fabulous. For once, Natalie appeared knocked off-balance. Her mouth flopped open, and Zen saw something she could use. "Honey, you have something on your teeth," she said sweetly. "What did you have for breakfast, seaweed?" Then she brushed past, exulting, as one of the queen bee's minions failed to suppress a laugh.

And then, lunch. Standing at the staging spot, she scanned the room.

Melissa at the clean-cut kids' table, giving her one look and then pointedly looking away. Fine, whatever. Things had been awkward again between them since the girls' night visit, and they had hardly talked all week.

Wire-Frame Glasses—Paul—gaping openly. Zen blinked and blushed slightly. And Robert at the same table, not looking at her in a careful, stagy way that had to be on purpose. The nod and smile in class had confused him, looked like.

And then, at Arli's table of orphan misfits, Arli, Clem, and Dyna, just like the first day, plus, for a bonus, Elijah. Zen's face bloomed into a grin and she hurried through the crowd to join them.

At the table, two conversations were happening at once. Dyna was giving Clem another French lesson, and Arli was talking earnestly to Elijah. Zen bent an ear to hear, assuming the conversation would be about gender, but it was not. It was about something much more important: fandoms. Elijah was leaning back a bit in the face of Arli's intensity, but answering, and one of the first words he said was "Kimazui."

Zen did a squee. "You're a Kimazui fan? Me too! I thought I was the only one in this whole school!" Then she got to see the shy boy smile for the first time. He had a sweet smile.

Clem took a break from practicing French to convey gossip. "Hey, did you hear?" he said. "They caught the hacker."

Dyna said, "It was announced in all the classes, I think."

"No, I mean, they found out who it was."

Arli and Zen exchanged an eyes-wide look. Keeping her voice light, Zen said, "Oh yeah? Who?"

Clem indulged in a suspenseful pause, then said, "He's sitting right over there. The hacker was our friend Chopper Robert." All eyes at the misfit table turned to the gamer table. Then a circle of looks back around their own table, and, seeing Zen and Arli's expressions, Clem faltered and said, "That's what I heard, anyway."

Arli and Zen conversed with their eyes. How to handle this? Arli said cautiously, "That might be just a rumor, I think."

The subject needed to be changed, and Zen remembered a happy piece of business. "Hey," she said. "Everyone. I have an important announcement. My Aunties are holding a Halloween party this weekend, and they said I could invite whoever I want."

"Yes!" said Arli, pumping veir fist.

"They really get into it, I guess, and have a lot of fun. So . . . wanna come over? Friday night, anytime from six o'clock on."

Arli, bouncing up and down, was clearly already ecstatic

about the invitation. Clem was smiling and nodding too. "I'll have to ask the 'rents, but I should be able to," he said.

Elijah's face had closed up, though, and Dyna looked troubled. She said, "Will someone there be drinking alcohol? If so, I do not think my father will give permission."

Zen said, "I don't know. I can ask." She turned to Elijah, pretty sure she knew the reason for his sudden walled-up expression. "And," she added, "if anyone starts to feel . . . leaned on . . . by all the people, there are a couple of quiet rooms to go into." After a few seconds, Elijah did a little nod and whispered, "I can ask."

"Good," said Zen. Still aware of the possibility of conversation getting back to the hacker, she shot Arli a look. Arli, reading it right, brought back the fandom thread by launching into a gush about veir favorite web comic, Novaglyph.

Once the subject-change was safely locked in, Zen's gaze wandered back to the clean-cut kids' table, and she wondered about asking Melissa to the Halloween party too. Even as her mind formed the question, though, she already knew the answer. Melissa was a kind girl in her way, but based on how she had responded to her mother's instruction about Elijah, Zen couldn't see how she could fit in at the party. Apparently some divides just couldn't be bridged. It was sad, but there it was. She turned back to the endless palaver of geekeries and fandoms, and, as lunch period passed, the talk looped and spun on, twining the individual spirals of the five young humans at the table into deeper interweavings of friendship.

INTERLUDE: SEEING ZEN

Aunt Lucy

Having Zenobia come into our home has thrown into stark relief the gap that exists in my life between theory and practice. I work with theory. I feel at home with theory. Real life, I confess, has always felt like more of a challenge than getting deep into ideas and working there.

But now here's Zenobia, who knows nothing whatsoever about -isms and -ologies. She is just alive, and trying as hard as she can with all her considerable strength to make sense of her life and to be who she is. It is often painful to watch, because she acts without thinking or just flails her way forward, but for all its human imperfection, her progress is also astonishing to witness. A testament to the power of the human will, even a very young one, when it bends itself unerringly to some difficult purpose.

Fair to say, I am a creature of routine, and Zen's presence in our lives has disrupted many routines. At times I have felt imposed upon, and I have sometimes in the privacy of my mind and heart yearned for the time before, or the time it will end. But when can that be? I haven't broached the subject with Phil yet—I need to meditate on it some more just by myself—but it is becoming increasingly clear to me that the only right thing to do is to adopt the child. To offer to, anyway, and to follow through if she wants to do it. We're only legal guardians right now. That emergency order. But she deserves a home. All children do.

And, beyond offering to adopt being the right thing, I just want to. Nothing theoretical about that part. I just do. Because I love her. She does things that make me crazy, but at this point I can't imagine life without her. What a ragged, painful hole she would leave if she went away. I don't know if I could bear it.

And anyway, she has nowhere else to go. Only us. So, yes, soon, there will be some more conversations, I think.

FIFTY-NINE

WHEN ZEN TOLD the Aunties that she had invited no fewer than four friends to their Halloween party there was a silence, and she experienced a moment of fear. Was she asking for too much? Would they pull back? But then they were enthusing about the opportunity to meet more of her friends, and she breathed again.

Not in the clear yet, though. A second moment of trepidation bringing up the issue of alcohol. Aunt Lucy, Zen had observed, relished the wine she sipped most evenings. The question asked, there was another silence to get through; but then Aunt Phil chucked and said, "I guess we're really finding out what it's like to be parents, now. The party hijack you can't refuse, and don't want to."

Hijack struck Zen as a scary word, and she endured one more moment of squirm before Aunt Lucy laughed and said, "It's going to come as a novelty to some of our other guests, but, sure, if it will help your friends feel welcome, we can make it alcohol-free."

By Friday afternoon it was confirmed that all four friends would be coming to the party. As the hour of first arrivals approached, Zen found herself unable to hold still, twitching when spoken to and laughing too hard at anything or nothing. Uncle Sprink was expected first, coming early to help Zen experiment with glam.

A little sooner than she felt ready, the doorbell rang. Zen opened the door and gasped. An enormous and magnificent woman stood in the foyer. The crown of her teased-up blond hair brushed the ceiling, and she was bedecked in an eye-dazzling expanse of gold lamé, a long purple feather boa, and spangly platform boots with heels at least four inches high. Her face, framed by huge hoop earrings, was a masterpiece of sculptural makeup artistry. The power-glam giantess stuck out one hip, threw her head back, and said in a sultry deep alto, "Hello, darling. Aren't you going to invite me in?"

It took Zen a second to unstick herself. She closed her hanging jaw and said, "Uncle . . . Uncle Sprink?"

"Call me Sprinkles, tonight, if you don't mind, love," said Sprinkles, stalking regally into the apartment. She turned and posed again. "I dressed completely before I came," she said, "because I thought you might like to see the full effect all at once. And because, every once in a while, I do enjoy walking the streets in full daylight. So: What do you think?"

Zen stammered, tried a couple of times to talk, and then blushed deeply.

Sprinkles said, "Darling, you're making me worry. Is

there something wrong with my look? Because I trust your judgment, and if it's not working, I'll change it."

Zen shook her head. "No, nothing's wrong," she said. "I think you look . . . I think you look absolutely amazing. I love it!"

"So what's the problem, sweetheart? Your face before . . . something was making you unhappy."

"Not you," Zen said. She groped for words. "Seriously, not you. It's just . . . Do you mind . . . Would it be okay if we don't do me the same? Because, now that I see, I don't think that's going to work for me. At all."

Sprinkles gave her an eyebrows-up frown. Zen couldn't tell whether it was real or put on. She tried again to explain. "Because . . . now that I see . . . I just don't think it would feel right. I don't want to be . . . a goddess. I just want to be me."

Sprinkles laughed at *goddess*. She tossed the feather boa back and said, "All right, sugar. No problem. We can figure something else out."

"Thank you," Zen said. Then she laughed too. "Arli is going to absolutely love you!"

When Aunt Phil understood a last-minute costume substitution was needed, she led Zen through the curtain into the Aunties' bedroom for some closet-rummaging. While that was going on, Zen noticed something she hadn't seen before: a black-and-white photograph on the dresser. She stepped close. Two women gazed out of the frame at her, caught at a tilt in a moment of laughter amidst action. It took Zen a moment to realize she was looking at her Aunties when they were younger.

Unlined faces. Strong white teeth. Fierce power shining out of their eyes. Behind her, Aunt Phil said, "Yep, that's us. Been a while."

Zen turned and looked at the older, much more worn face before her. What had this person seen? What had she lived through? Zen suddenly felt very young, and a bit abashed. "You look . . . um . . . so alive," she said.

Aunt Phil liked that. "Yep," she said. "Then, and now, and all the time in between getting from there to here. The endless dance."

They shared a smile, then got back to rummaging. Aunt Phil stopped at a rough homespun-cloth skirt dyed in colorful rainbow stripes. She pulled it out and held it up, her brow wrinkled. "Well now," she said. "Funny, finding this, right after looking at that picture. Do you like it?"

Zen nodded.

"Wear this, you could be an Aquarian. A flower child."

Zen nodded again, feeling the wanting-to rise up in her.

"It's Lu's. Hold on a second." Aunt Phil turned to the archway and called, "Lu!"

Aunt Lucy came in, wearing the suit and tie that were her getup for the night. "Yes?" she said.

Aunt Phil held up the skirt. Zen said tentatively, "For my costume? I was thinking maybe I could be a flower child?"

Aunt Lucy stepped forward and fingered the fabric of the skirt. "My goodness," she said. Her face had gone thoughtful, almost sad. "I didn't know I still had that." Her eyes came to

Zen's, and she said, "I wore this skirt when we marched after Harvey Milk was shot. Do you know who he was?"

Zen looked down at the floor and said, "I'm sorry, no."

"He was one of the most important . . . Yes, you know, now is perhaps not the best time for a history lesson. It can wait. You'll learn." Zen remained mute. A silence. Then Aunt Lucy, with a touch of roughness in her voice, said, "Zenobia. My dear Zen. If you would like to have this skirt, I would be honored to pass it on to you."

Zen looked up again, eyes wide. "Oh! Um . . . well, that's really . . . What I mean is, if you want to give it to me, I would be honored to receive it. Thank you."

Aunt Lucy smiled. "Good." Were those agate eyes moist? Zen's certainly were. Impulsively, she darted forward and hugged her tall aunt, who, more quickly and naturally than other times, hugged back. From the embrace Zen glanced at Aunt Phil, who looked on, smiling. Zen realized something, and said, "You're not wearing a costume?"

Aunt Phil ran her hand through her red-orange-yellow crest, then back along the close-shaved gray sides. Her fingers brushed the many earrings. "Honeybunch, I'm kinda sorta always in costume," she said.

SIXTY

A FLURRY OF flower-girl-outfit construction, with makeup help from Sprinkles, topped off by the Grandma Gail earrings. On final inspection, the cross pendant looked out of place, so she detached the chain, lowered the cross gently onto the little table by her bed, and pooled the chain over and around it. The doorbell rang. Zen ran to open it. Arli and Clem stood on the front porch, and Dyna could be seen walking up the block behind them.

Giddy greetings, introductions, inquiries about costumes. Arli's needed explaining—a character from veir web comic. Clem had done a half vampire, half werewolf. Dyna had found a hijab with cat's ears. The bell rang again, and Elijah was there, dressed as a used-car salesman, with a loud checked jacket and a plastic cigar.

And then the happy hubbub of a good party in full swing was happening all around. Arli, as Zen had predicted, immediately attached veirself to Sprinkles. Aunt Lucy began a conversation with Dyna, reminding her of their mall encounter. Aunt Phil was being kind to Elijah, coaxing him farther in with talk of treats in the kitchen. The bell rang again, and other Auntie-friends joined them. Someone turned on the radio. The DJ on WYZA was playing wacky old Halloween songs.

Half an hour in, Zen suddenly felt her chest go tight. Alarmed, she retreated to the bathroom and closed the door. She leaned against it and worked to get her breath back. It didn't matter who the other people were—when the introvert buffers were full, they were full.

As her body began to unclench she tuned in to the voices on the other side of the door. She heard Clem's bizarre laugh, mixed with Aunt Phil's deep chuckle. She heard the distinctive rhythm and cadence of Aunt Lucy explaining something. Closer, she heard Arli say distinctly, "Ex. Cell. Ent!" In the background, other voices chattered and laughed.

Zen drew a shuddery breath, surprised by a sudden uprush of happiness so intense it hurt. The lovely humans on the other side of the door: they were there because of her. She had brought them together. She connected them all. And, just for this moment, she was apart but close, listening to them find each other.

A tear pooled at the corner of her eye. Solicitous of makeup artistry, she blotted it carefully with a tissue. Then, with the least amount of fear she could recall feeling since moving to this new place and life, she faced the mirror.

All girl? Meh? Maybe? Her eyes ran the gamut of problem spots, and, yeah, when she looked for them, she could see them. But for once it didn't seem to matter. She was in costume, among welcoming hearts. At least for this little stretch of time, it felt safe to stop thinking about how she looked to the world. For once it felt like she could just be.

Zenobia July took in and blew out three long breaths. She smiled at herself in the mirror, then smiled more at how pretty the smile was. She checked her costume one more time. She reached up and gently touched the beautiful old earrings her grandmother had given her. Then she put her shoulders back, lifted her chin, turned to the door, opened it, and stepped back out among the people she loved, to be with them and one of them, into the warmth and music and joy of what was starting to feel very much like a family.